Praise for Susan Trott's

THE HOLY MAN and THE HOLY MAN'S JOURNEY

"Endlessly entertaining and gently profound."

- Kirkus Reviews

"Reminiscent of Chaucer's Canterbury Tales, The Holy Man dispenses a fresh brand of wisdom. With wit and modern insight, it compels readers to look inward, to turn to themselves, for enlightenment."

- Booklist

"The simplicity of her tale and the lucidity of her writing make this novel a major contender in the inspirational self-help field."

- Library Journal

"Throughout, Trott's inventive mind and playful characterizations surprise us."

- San Francisco Chronicle

"Tolerance, overcoming greed and ignorance, recognizing the inherent holiness of people and nature - shines through Trott's prose."

- Publisher's Weekly

"A sincere and earnest fable ... a particular brand of spirituality where old and new jibe in mutual tolerance and kindness. Westernized Buddhism mingles freely with Christianity."

- Los Angleles Times

"Trott has written a wise and warmhearted book."

- Pacific Sun

"The Holy man is infused with gentle bits of good sense and admonitions of brotherly and sisterly love."

- The Arizona Star

"Charming, with much wisdom between its pages."

- The Calgary Herald

"One of the most exquisitely beautiful books to be written in years."

- Ocala Star-Banner

"Trott is as wily as her sweet-spirited holy man, using her no-pressure storytelling style to lull readers into unexpected moments of wit and illumination."

- Publisher's Weekly

"Susan Trott's parabolic gem shines with insights into the relationship between teachers and disciples. It also reveals that the world is a school for our enlightenment. The Holy Man's Journey is so simple and so profound that we can hardly wait for the next instalment."

- Values and Visions

Book Descriptions

Book 1: The Holy Man

In a hermitage at the top of a mountain lives the Holy Man. Every summer a trail of pilgrims queues at the hermitage gates and each pilgrim is hoping for words of wisdom from the Holy Man that will heal their lives.

There is the impatient woman who learns peace, the jealous man who learns trust, the famous man who learns humility and the guilty mercenary who finds a mission. In each of the many characters we can see mirrored something of ourselves. Some learn their lessons from other pilgrims, some from the holy man himself; others find answers from the experience of being on the mountain. These stories unravel the knots of everyday anxieties with profound ease, humor, wisdom, and elegance. Perhaps the most winning feature of this book is that we're all in here, somewhere, with our wounded egos, insecurities, bad tempers, impatience and ambitiousness. The Holy man shows us the good we already have in us but cannot see.

Book 2: The Holy Man's Journey

The Holy Man became a national best seller. Now, The Holy Man's Journey picks up the story of the great wise man. Joe has recognized Anna as his successor. She and her troublesome husband, Errol, and their two children, are staying at the hermitage. Joe decides he must take Anna on a trip to visit his former teacher, Chen, at his Universe-city. Joe's health is failing and Anna is concerned that the trip will be too much for him. As it turns out, Joe knows exactly what he's doing. He uses the journey as a learning experience for Anna and as a spiritual cure for his corrupted mentor. It is a journey which brings enlightenment to Anna and a spiritual cure to Chen.

Intimate and revealing, this is a tale of friendship and love that shows the human side of the holy man while never ceasing to instruct and enlighten the reader.

THE
HOLY WOMAN

Book Three of the
HOLY MAN TRILOGY

by
SUSAN TROTT

Outskirts Press, Inc.
Denver, Colorado

This is a work of fiction. The events and characters described herein are imaginary and are not intended to refer to specific places or living persons. The opinions expressed in this manuscript are solely the opinions of the author and do not represent the opinions or thoughts of the publisher. The author has represented and warranted full ownership and/or legal right to publish all the materials in this book.

The Holy Woman
Book Three of the Holy Man Trilogy
All Rights Reserved.
Copyright © 2009 Susan Trott
v3.0

This book may not be reproduced, transmitted, or stored in whole or in part by any means, including graphic, electronic, or mechanical without the express written consent of the publisher except in the case of brief quotations embodied in critical articles and reviews.

Outskirts Press, Inc.
http://www.outskirtspress.com

ISBN: 978-1-4327-4418-2

Outskirts Press and the "OP" logo are trademarks belonging to Outskirts Press, Inc.

PRINTED IN THE UNITED STATES OF AMERICA

Chapter 1
Joe's Burial

They couldn't bury the holy man anywhere around the hermitage because the ground was too rocky so they found a place a quarter of a mile down the back path of the mountain, the one the pilgrims would use for their downward departure after seeing the holy man. The burial spot was a place where Joe had liked to lie down and and look at the sky to watch clouds form, dissolve, be threaded by birds.

Anna, stood with her husband, Errol, and their children: Melissa, who was almost four, and Jimmy, almost six. The Korean marathoner, Kim, he who had been most like a son to Joe, was next to Ho, the Chinese cellist, probably Joe's closest friend and the four other monks were there along with Jacob who, feeling unworthy of monk-hood, termed himself the holy bodyguard. All these dearest friends were gathered together for Joe's burial; grieving but no longer weeping as almost a week had passed since his death.

There had been a memorial service in the town park below, with all the children he had rejoiced to play with whenever he traversed the ten miles down the mountain, and with the townspeople who were the grown children he had played with in years past; since Joe had lived among them in this foreign land for thirty years. Many of his monks from the past had flown in from various nations to honor Joe's passing. This, the actual burial ceremony, the current monks had reserved for themselves. And Chen.

Chen, Joe's teacher who, with Anna, had brought back Joe's body on his private jet, had remained for the funeral, busy man though he was, with all of his Universe-city to preside over.

Anna, looking at Chen had the barbarous thought that Jesus had died for all mankind but Joe, seemingly, had died for Chen, who, by the way, wasn't worth it. Well, he would be worth it if he would now turn his wisdom and fantastic charisma to the good of the world rather than to the expansion of his city and his car collection. Chen, like Joe, could be a force for peace and understanding among people, only more widespread, since he wasn't averse to modern methods of communication and people flocked to him in stadiums as to a rock star. Whereas Joe had dropped his nectar of guidance into people's ears one by one.

Jacob, who was considered the holy bodyguard by the others because of his towering strength, his steadfast loyalty, his willingness to brave anything for them, was doing most of the shoveling along with Errol and Kim.

Tens of thousands of his followers would be there, too, if they knew about his demise. However, when Joe and Anna had gone off on their journey to save Chen, Joe had decreed a sign be posted at the bottom of the mountain's path, "The Holy Man Is Gone", so that those legions who came to see him each summer would not climb the mountain in vain. The word had spread throughout the world that he was no longer at the hermitage and soon it would spread that he was part of the universe. Would the word spread that Anna had taken his place?

The beautiful coffin Chen had his carpenter contrive was lowered into the hole and soon covered with flowers and dirt. No one spoke any words because there was nothing more to say. They all felt gratitude for having known Joe. Each monk, from his position of eminence, had spread the holy man's message that everyone was a holy person and should be treated as such, that everyone had the potential to make a contribution to the world in a small or large way.

Ho played a composition of his own that was elegiac but not mournful, strains that were playful, as the holy man himself had been playful. It was almost a dance. The boulder birds came, as Anna expected, aligning themselves on the boulder's summits, singing along with Ho's cello. Joe's favorite blue flowers, lupin, seemed to crowd to the edge of the raw earth as if longing to cover his grave with their sweetness and splendor.

When Ho's piece was finished, raindrops began to fall from out of the pure blue sky, like minuscule drops of silver, sparkles almost, glimmers, not wetting them at first, only covering them, making them all shine, making them laugh and touch each other. "Joe's last trick," they said, while Anna and Chen looked at each other knowing that the holy man's last trick had been in the dying itself.

Then it turned to rain in earnest, hard rain, and although it wasn't cold, the usual mild panic set in when rain comes and ruins an occasion. There was concern for Ho's valuable instrument and Kim ran for the case that had been left at the Hermitage while the monks made a tent around it of their bodies. The fleet Kim soon had it properly enclosed then the rain doubled and redoubled in force, causing the mountain springs to gush forth and run rampant. The sky was now an eggplant-purple with bolts of lightening jittering down like intricate roots of fire. Thunderclaps replaced the haunting cello music, rolling like freight trains. They all ran for the hermitage, splashing through water and mud, dodging the rocks which were coming loose from the downpour of rain and the upsurge of spring water. The bigger rocks, the boulders, toppled and rolled, carving gouges down the mountain's slopes, making new runways for the overabundance of water. This storm went on for the rest of the day and all of the night.

What happened in the end was that the mountain rearranged itself. Nothing was quite where it had been before. Both paths to the hermitage were obliterated. The hermitage itself was partially destroyed., only the kitchen and common room remaining in any sort of usable fashion.

Afterward, no one could ever find the holy man's grave.

Chapter 2
Not a Holy Woman

"A fresh beginning, I guess," said Anna, the morning after the storm when they were gathered in the common room having a fitful breakfast, after bewildered forays out and about surveying the damage. She affected a brave face as she scanned the storm-wrecked rooms, but was unable to hide her deep dismay.

"I am inviting you all to return with me to my Universe-city," said Chen, where you can regroup. I want you all to see what I am doing there."

"And what you will be doing there," Anna reminded him.

"Yes. My city where now, thanks to Joe's intervention, birth, old age and death will be welcome."

This cheered Anna. Maybe Joe's death would not be in vain. As it stood now, Chen's creation of a city of eternal life was a masterpiece of delusion.

"It was a place only for the young, the healthy and the beautiful," Anna explained to the others.

"Sounds great to me," Ed said, laughing.

"Yes," said Chen smoothly. "I have put into practice certain ideas for immortality which I will not abandon but which I will temper." He smiled at Anna. His raven hair shone and his eyes glittered as if still containing the silver of yesterday's shower. He, himself, embodied all that was young and healthy and beautiful although Anna knew he must be well into his fifties. She considered him a dangerous man although part of Joe's teaching on their journey was not to be judgmental, especially of Chen, no matter what she saw and heard respecting him. Joe honored Chen to the last.

"Will you accept my invitation?" His glance included them all. His smile was hypnotically charming. "My jet awaits at the airport and there is plenty of room for all."

"It seems right," said Marie, that we should honor Joe's passing by spending time with his teacher, the fount of his knowledge."

"Yes, yes," everyone seemed dazzled into

immediate agreement. They all turned to each other, saying, "Let's spend time with Joe's teacher. What could be more appropriate?"

The teacher Joe parted from twenty five years ago, Anna thought, whom he returned to at the last only because he knew Chen had become completely deranged and needed his help. But I can't vie for Joe's monks. They must follow their own path and if Chen wants to play the Pied Piper and woo them all away, I am helpless.

Anna spoke these words to herself in a feisty manner but her heart was sinking fast. What was she going to do? Would anyone stick by her? She didn't want this last assembly to be unpleasant as happens when people die and their families wrangle over the will, citing dubious verbal promises of the deceased.

Ho spoke. "We all know that Joe chose Anna to continue his work, to be the new holy one to whom pilgrims would come for answers to their problems and suffering. I think I speak for us all when we say that we love Anna and abide by Joe's love for her but feel that he was overcome by his own feelings as his health failed, that he saw in Anna his own lost wife, or his daughter as she would be had she lived and grown to Anna's age."

"Yes, yes," everyone murmured, suddenly recognizing, or wanting desperately to believe, that Anna was nothing more than a chimera of Joe's, a creature of his faltering imagination - as if, thought Anna, Joe ever faltered over anything! "Not that we think he should have chosen one of us, just that we think ...well, that it is over now. Joe is gone. The hermitage is in shambles. The storm has spoken."

Mutiny! Anna thought. Monk mutiny. She said. "Do I think I can replace Joe? Certainly not. Our journey together was a learning trip and I mostly learned how unenlightened I am but he chose me, he did. I will dedicate my life to Joe's legacy. I will do my best."

"Won't you come with us to Chen's?" Kim pleaded, coming to Anna's side and embracing her. Kim was the youngest of them all and the sweetest. She was warmed by Kim's embrace and blinked back tears but, as to returning to Chen's empire, she responded, "Never!"

Chen smiled. He understood her completely.

Kim was dismayed. "Please don't leave us, Anna," as if unaware that they were the ones leaving her.

Errol entered the room during this last exchange. "Anna will come home to Ireland with me and the kids. This lunacy has gone on long enough. And it has ended in tragedy. Joe has died and now the hermitage we all worked so hard on this spring to restore and improve, is virtually demolished. "

"It's like the mountain is saying, Get off me!" Helena added with a flourish.

"No," said Anna. "The mountain was saying to Joe, Get in me. It was the mountain's way of putting him deep inside. It will be a magic mountain from now on. Just by setting ones foot on the mountain one will be healed of all ills. Joe always felt that was part of the process, the pilgrim's difficult climb, their experiencing nature, some for the first time, sleeping under the stars, socializing with the other pilgrims ..."

"Good. Then you agree you don't need to stay," said Errol interrupting brusquely.

"I answered the holy man's call when it came to me in my dreams. I came to him then left, putting my family first. Jacob came and got me because the holy man was alone and dying. You and Jimmy and Melissa came, bringing joy to his last year on earth. Then he took me on his final journey, anointing me. My place is here, if nothing else, as .. as holy custodian." She felt her chin lifting defiantly and almost had to laugh at herself.

Was Chen looking at her with approval? If so, he was the only one.

"Mom's 'nointed," said Melissa who had been hanging on every word. Jimmy nodded. So they approved, too. And Jacob, of course would believe in her. She didn't even need to look at him to know the holy bodyguard would stay by her side.

"We are the Anna-Kerchiefians, don't forget," Jimmy reminded them, and indeed they all were adorned one way or another with the colorful kerchief Anna had instigated and designed. The words, "It's good luck to be nice," were printed in the pattern.

"Oh, give me a break," said Errol, throwing up his hands.

"Errol's right that your family should come first," said Henri.

Have your families come first? Anna wanted to ask them all but then the discussion would degenerate into bickering. The hermitage had been a place primarily of silence. Bickering was beyond the pale.

She said calmly, "If he wishes, Errol can return to his work and leave the children with me but we must talk about that, just the two of us. You monks will go with Chen. I'll remain here as Joe wanted."

Everyone packed their knapsacks, everyone

but Errol and Jacob who would attend the others down the ravaged landscape and then return to Anna and the children. Jacob had remained quiet throughout the discussion, as was his way.

The monks said their warm farewells and Anna worked very hard not to feel they were deserting her. Joe's philosophy had always been to let his monks go, to make them go. He never wanted followers, only people who would go forth from him and be examples of love, peace, and truth. It was the abruptness of their departure that hurt her so much even though she knew it was not their fault, but orchestrated by Chen.

Chen took her hand in his. She could feel the incredible electricity. She knew he would say something profound in parting and tried to open herself to his words rather than steel herself against them.

Chen had been with them for five days and they all had fallen under his influence. He was a genius. He was glorious to look upon. He made one feel important, blessed. She was a small, thin, Irish woman, thirty four years old, with only her red hair to distinguish her.

"Yes, you are ordinary," Chen said.

Even his telling her she was ordinary made her

feel important and blessed, as if ordinariness was rare, seldom come upon in a world full of extraordinary people. Now she felt that Chen, too, had anointed her, chosen her, although to do what was unclear.

Anna watched them all go with eager steps. Only Kim turned with a last smile and a wave.

Chapter 3
All Right

When they had gone, Anna went off to try not to cry about the monks' desertion. With Melissa and Jimmy trailing after her, she picked her way downhill until she found herself in what she believed to be the vicinity of Joe's grave on the transfigured mountain. The sound of rushing water was all around her for although it no longer fell from the sky, it realized itself in a tangle of streams, rivulets, bog and sog. The children fell to making mud pies or, in Jimmy's case, mud balls to throw and splatter on the rocks.

Anna found one of the boulders that was on a new tilt and sat herself down. "They're gone Joe. Can you believe it? They all just up and left. Not Jacob of course. And Errol and the kids are still here but Errol, who I thought had resigned himself to stay is now talking serious departure action. Joe I miss you so much. I didn't know what to say to anyone. I floundered. I babbled. Only Melissa seemed to agree with me that I was 'nointed by you and should carry on your work. Chen gave me his card when he left. I was hard put not to spit on it, crumple it, then put it under my feet and do a Russian dance on it. The awful thing is I feel I'll need Chen one day and that I shouldn't burn my bridges. Anyhow, I will stay on at the half-hermitage, at least for the summer. Joe you should see the mountain today. It is back to its wild self. It's as it was when you first climbed it to build your original hut. It positively gleams. It's funny, I came to your grave-vicinity with the idea of trying with all my might not to cry and find instead I am trying not to laugh! I feel full of joy and hope, Joe. Not just because I feel I will be all right but because I feel the world will be, too.

Chapter 4
Giving

Anna heard Errol shouting for her. "Anna, where are you?"

"Here!"

Slipping, sliding, barely recovering his balance each time, he ran toward her. "I was walking down the mountain with the others, helping them find the way – you can't imagine the storm damage, it's a mine field – and I talked a lot with Chen. He's persuaded me to come with them. He found out I'm an architect and his city is full of architectural marvels. Also, he wants my advice on a new building."

Errol's face was alight as she had not seen it for a long time. He, too, was feeling that sense of renewal and hope, of all-rightness.

Anna's generous heart burst out with the response. "But of course, my darling. You must go. You will love to see that marvelous place."

"It's a possible job, too."

"Good. Your talent has lain fallow this year outside of making adobe bricks for the hermitage and piling them into walls."

"When I come back, we will talk about what to do with ourselves."

"Yes, this will be a time for thinking."

"I will write to you care of Ezla or Alim," he named two of their friends in the town below: Ezla who was the ceramic pot maker, and Alim, the owner of the photography shop.

"Do."

"I've got to run to catch up with them all."

"I understand"

He embraced her and she felt his lithe, strong body against hers, his body that was always a balm for her emotionally and physically. They'd been together since they were teenagers, together as she went to nursing school, he to university. Errol was on his way to a successful career in a Galway firm when she brought disruption to their life. But it was such a good disruption for them all and now, for Errol, the signs were good. "Say goodbye to the children."

He went to the children and swung them around. He gave them hugs and kisses. He was a good father. All the pent-up anger he'd been carrying around recently (and, really, for most of his life) seemed dispelled by the voodoo of Chen who had now taken her husband away from her as well as the monks. She wondered if Jacob would return from the downhill trek and knew that he would, no question. Why couldn't she have the same trust in Errol. She wanted to and yet, when she had returned with Joe's body five days ago, she learned that Errol had come very close to leaving with the children while she was away. She remembered the despair that had swept over her – her blackest moment.

"You'll be all right with Jacob," Errol said, perhaps feeling some guilt, perhaps not.

"I am all right with only myself," Anna said, lifting her chin (again). "But, Errol, although this is a great chance for you, keep your wits about you with Chen."

He smiled, kissed her goodbye, promised to keep in constant touch, and plunged down the precipitous path.

"I mean I'm all right with myself and the children," she shouted after him, afraid she had given him licence to take the children away with him next time. How she rued those words of false bravado, I'm all right with only myself. Pride was one of the three poisons along with anger and greed. In one morning she had experienced two of them – anger at Chen, then pride in her strength to overcome rejection by the others. At least she was free of greed, unless wanting everyone to stay with her was being greedy. It probably was. They all had their own lives to live. Who would forego a chance to be with Chen? Joe himself had said Chen was one of the company of great prophets – Buddha, Lao-tsu, Jesus, Confucius.

So far, I have been generous, she told herself. If I start to resent Errol and the others, my generosity is undone. I am truly glad to see that light of happiness in Errol's eyes. It is a light I can no longer bring to them.

"Daddy is happy," Melissa said.

"I hope he doesn't fall down the mountain," said Jimmy.

"I gave him my kerchief so he'll remember us," Melissa said.

Tears sprang to Anna's eyes. After a minute to collect herself, she said, "That was sweet of you. We'll find another one for you."

"Then I can give it to someone else," Melissa frowned her little brow, "Giving is fun. It's part of being nice, which is lucky. But I shouldn't have a reason, should I."

"What do you mean?"

"Next time when I give away a kerchief, I'll tell the person, you don't have to remember us."

This is why Joe loved being with children, Anna thought.

Chapter 5
Another Departure

Jacob returned at evening time, his knapsack full of dried fruits, nuts, some fresh vegetables, and coffee. There still were bags of rice, dried milk, and flour in the larder. There was fresh spring water outside. They would have enough nourishment for a while.

Jacob was a man in his sixties. His granite-like face and body were beginning to, not sag but yield, to age and to the constant sorrow he carried for his misspent life. He had devoted himself to Anna since the day they had met in the line to the holy man, then devoted himself also to the holy man and his monks as he became part of the community, but he would always feel an outsider. He had been a murderer.

Joe, too, had been a warrior as had Ho. They had served their countries and could say, did say to Jacob, that they, too, had blood on their hands. But Jacob, as a boy, had joined the French Foreign Legion. It was a different kind of killing, mercenary, not for God or Country. Afterward, still drunk on blood, he'd been an assassin for one country or another. Finally he'd gone back to Austria and pulled his life together. He'd become a successful business man, a millionaire. No one knew of his past. It was deeply buried (and festering). He had married and had children. More than once. Then he'd become depressed. He thought constantly of the boys he'd killed who never got to live the splendid life he had, or any life. He feared his violent nature might reassert itself. He was afraid to hurt someone and he was sure he would hurt himself. On the verge of suicide, he had sought out the holy man, confessed everything, and been saved.

"Before I left Austria the last time," he told Anna, as they drank their coffee after dinner, "I gave all my money to my three sons, keeping just enough for my daily bread. Joe of course would never take money from anyone or I'd have given it all to him. Now I am thinking I'd better go back home and try to recapture some funds for you and me and the children. Possibly Errol will be sending some money but I rather suspect Chen doesn't pay people for the honor of working for him. More likely, they pay him."

Jacob looked around. "I won't leave right away. I want to make the hermitage safe from its storm damage. I have just enough money left for my ticket. You will be fine without me. It will only be a matter of weeks."

She smiled. "The children and I will be fine ." She didn't need to lift her chin. She meant it.

Jacob left a week later. Melissa looked at him with big eyes as she gave him her new kerchief. "You don't need to remember us," she said.

Jacob laughed as he tied the kerchief around his neck. "I certainly don't need to remember three people whose images are engraved on my heart."

"What does that mean, graved on your heart? Are we buried there?"

"You are alive there, little one, causing my heart to beat its sixty times a minute. Here, Feel."

She put her tiny hand on his massive chest. "If we died would your heart stop beating, Uncle Jacob?"

"Yes, it would."

"Now Jacob, don't say such things. You will

frighten her. Melissa, Jacob was saying he doesn't need anything to remember you by because he loves you so much. We don't forget people we love."

Anna thought sadly that if by some horrible chance Jacob did not return to their lives, Melissa, only three years old, would forget him. And yet, knowing that it is the first years that inform the years to come, all those good Jacobian seeds of strength and kindness would be sprouting all her life.

Just as dim in her memory would be a little old man, a saint, who had held her in his arms, laughed with her, told her stories. Already taken root in her tiny body, already invading her with goodness and honor, was Joe's legacy.

Jacob went away down the mountain that no longer had a trail and Anna, Melissa, and Jimmy were left alone in the half-hermitage which Jacob had made as snug for them as he could.

Chapter 6
Spendthrift

It was a shock for Jacob to be back in Austria after his months on the mountain. The industry, traffic, lights, noise, masses of people buffeted him about. He knew he'd get back in the swing of it, but meanwhile he was reeling.

He had determined to go to each of his sons to see how they had done with the million dollars he had given them and ask for a small return of his investment in them to help out his friends on the mountain.

"You must check into a hotel," said his eldest son, Franz. "We are redecorating here and you would have to wade through paint cans and swatches of material, not to mention all the worker bees."

It was Franz who had taken over Jacob's department stores. "Business is bad," he told his father, when they met at a café. "I'm cutting back. I've closed five of the stores and am just keeping the three in the biggest cities. I don't have the Midas touch that you had," he said defensively as if it were Jacob's fault not to have passed that on as well. As if he had purposely held back the most important ingredient in the recipe.

Including his time with Joe and Anna and his previous travels, Jacob only had been gone a little over two years and was appalled at the news. But he hadn't come to criticize, he'd come to beg.

Franz was a shorter man than his father and although only forty years old had turned fat in a burly rotund way so that one felt if he fell over, he'd roll away. He took his father to his house for dinner in his black Mercedes sedan. "Wait until you see my house. It's magnificent. I built it with the money you gave me." Franz sighed. "Of course, the contractors underbid and it cost a good deal more than I expected. They sued me for extra costs. For some reason I forgot I'd have to furnish it and by the time my wife was done shopping, its furnishing cost almost as much as the house. Then, with such a house, one has to entertain, and so Ava needed a new wardrobe. Designer dresses. One minute I'm a millionaire and before the year is out I'm deeply in debt. Even closing the stores hasn't made a difference in what I can take away from the business. I hope you will advise me what to do. I would be deeply ashamed to declare bankruptcy but it might be the only answer."

The house was ghastly, as were his wife's dresses and decorating schemes. Jacob relinquished any hopes of getting money from that son. He gave up three weeks of his time to shore up his son's affairs so that he could skate by for at least another year. He did this because he felt he had not done his son a favor to give him such a huge sum when he had not learned properly how to handle money. In trepidation, he went on to the middle son.

Chapter 7
Miser

Karl had not spent any of the money his father gave him. He'd invested it in stocks, bonds, and mutual funds and now he watched it. He watched it on his computer, day and night, when he wasn't talking on the phone to his broker. Karl had his father's athletic build but now he was thin and flaccid. His face was pale, his skin dry, his hair lank. He lived in small apartment that was not nice, not even very clean.

"My wife left me," he complained. "I have to pay her alimony and child support." Jacob could see that this caused him unbearable pain, not her having left him, but his having to pay the money. "I've hired lawyers to try to evade it but I can't. This money you gave me isn't her money. I kept it in my name. But I still have to pay her."

"If you were working, you could pay her that money," Jacob suggested. "And invest the other."

"I am working. This is work that I do here, tending to my finances."

"Are you well ahead?"

"No! Not with having to pay her and the children and fill my own small needs."

"And of course there are the lawyers and brokers to pay," Jacob nodded understandingly.

"And the taxes!"

"Of course. The taxes. Karl, my son, I am very sorry I gave you this money. Two years ago you were a happily married man. You liked your job as a social worker. You played soccer on weekends. You took the family skiing ..."

Karl didn't hear what Jacob was saying. "I am just about keeping even," he said with a hint of pride. "Despite all my expenses, I still have close to the original million, but it takes every second of my time."

"Karl, you have become a miser."

"What? One of those people who keep their gold under their bed and count it every night?" He laughed. "Not me. I am using my money."

"To do what?"

"Why, to make more! And do you see what has

happened to Franz. It is terrible. You never should have given Franz that money. He spends it like there's no tomorrow. If only he'd let me manage it for him."

"What about Bertil?" Jacob asked about the youngest son.

"I don't see much of Bertil. Franz has seen him, though. Bertil loaned him some money, quite a lot. Bertil's a fool."

Jacob stayed a few days with Karl, trying to make him see what his life had become, that he no longer had a life. But he could not make an impression and, again, the purpose of his visit was not to condemn the handling of their money, only to try to get a little back. However, he felt he had better not ask for any of his million back fro Karl for fear it would trigger a heart attack – or a patricide.

Chapter 8
Fool

Bertil had a house in the country in a small village by the river. It was a relief for Jacob to get out of the city and feel some earth under his feet, see the stars at night. His son lived with a girl friend and some other friends in a house full of music and paintings and colorful furnishings, surrounded by a wildly beautiful garden. He had a second-hand bookstore full of villagers drinking coffee and gossiping but rarely, it seemed, buying books. It turned out Bertil had loaned his money to others as well as to Franz, even to people he hardly knew.

"Yes, Dad, I made a mess of it. It's about all gone. Luckily I bought this little shop. I'd always wanted my own book store. It doesn't look like much but buyers come from the cities looking for first editions. I've got a good eye for finding them in the most unexpected places and I love going off with Magda on my book hunts. So, you could say I came out ahead. Some of our friends who stay with us are writing books so, who knows, maybe I'm fostering another Thomas Mann or Carl Handke."

"Yes, maybe you are."

"Gee, Dad, it's great to see you. Tell me what you've been doing these last years."

He was the first son to inquire. Jacob described a little of his activities.

"Well, you look wonderful."

"You do too, Bertil. You have used the money best of all by giving it all away. I have to admit, I came home, hoping to recover some, as I have a little family to support , not my own, mind you, but friends who, like you, I am fostering."

"Surely I can find some money for you, Dad. There are always ways. I could get a mortgage on the shop."

"No, although I thank you with all my heart for that offer."

Jacob spent some happy days with Bertil then left him, saying, "I am proud of you. You're a good boy. I love you."

"I love you too. Come and see me again. You're

always welcome."

Jacob went away from Bertil, just as poor as before, but happy that one son was thriving. Then Jacob feared he had showed favoritism to Bertil. He should tell the other two that he loved them and was proud of them because that's what parents do. They say it to their children when they are little but forget to say it when they are grown, when their belief in themselves may be faltering.

Had he ever said it to them when they were little?

Jacob went back to Karl to say, "I forgot to tell you you're a good boy. I'm proud of you and I love you."

"Really?"

"Yes."

"You don't think I'm a miser after all?"

"Yes, I do, but I love you anyway and I believe you will see your way to a good life."

"I've been thinking about what you said, about my not having a life. If I asked my wife to come back ...?

"That would be very good," Jacob smiled.

"Yes. Then I could save on the alimony and child support and really get ahead."

"Perhaps so. Goodbye, again." Jacob said, not

releasing his heavy sigh until he was well away.

He went back to his oldest son, Franz. "Everything is in good order," Franz said. "If I can only get Ava to stop splurging, I think I will be okay. I have told her we'll lose everything if she doesn't stop shopping but she says she can't."

"You can never get her to stop, son. She will have to want to stop."

"Yes, I see."

"Good luck, then. I love you. And I'm proud that you are trying to get your life in order." Despite himself, Jacob couldn't resist giving advice. "You had better consider scaling back, perhaps selling the house."

"I could never do that."

"No, you will have to want to."

Chapter 9
The Gambler

As his time away extended itself, Jacob left messages with Alim for Anna. He hated to go back to the mountain empty-handed and thought he would try one last thing. He returned to young Bertil. "Bertil, let's try to call in one of your loans. I'll go and talk to the person myself. Who would you suggest is the best bet?"

"I loaned ten thousand to an old classmate of mine. He hadn't been a particular friend but he heard I'd come into the money. He had gambling debts and was afraid for his life. I couldn't say no. He swore he'd never gamble again."

It didn't sound hopeful but Jacob gave it a try. He found the man living in his Volkswagen van. It was neat and clean but perhaps only because there was nothing left for the man to sell. He had the hunted look gamblers have when they're not laying on the charm. As he had with his sons, Jacob found himself caring about the man and his situation more than getting the money from him. This was the holy man's legacy. A few years ago, he would have wrung the man's neck until he came up with what he owed.

"Yes, your son, Bertil, bailed me out in the nick of time so I don't have any broken knees. But did I stop gambling? No. I felt lucky to have escaped, so I felt I should try my luck and it held. I went on a wonderful streak of winning and living high off the hog." He smiled happily, then was struck with remorse. "I should have paid Bertil back then, right? But, truth is, I completely forgot about the loan. Maybe if I'd paid him back my luck would have held, but I began to lose and so you see me here, living as I do in this field, out of my car, no better than a homeless person, and I am from good family, like Bertil. Could you help me out?"

Jacob didn't tell him that he was a homeless person, too. The difference was, he didn't feel homeless. He was still a strong man and could get any kind of job any time. Now he realized that was exactly what he would do. He would go back to the holy man's mountain and get a job in the town.

So, on second thought, he did tell the gambler his situation. "I am homeless, too. I gave my money away to my sons and went to live in a monastery. Now the monastery has folded and since I have failed to recover this money my son loaned you, I shall return to the country where I live now and get a job. Why don't you get a job too?"

"What a novel idea. I haven't worked for years. But I still have a brain. In fact my gambling has kept my mind active. I'm good at math."

"Go and see my oldest son, Franz. He will find something for you in the department store. Attend one of those gamblers anonymous meetings. Perhaps it will help you shed this poison that has enveloped you."

The gambler's face lit up. "Can you just give me enough money for a new suit so I can make a good appearance in front of Franz?"

"Don't make me laugh," Jacob said.

Chapter 10
The Kerchief

"I have learned," Jacob told Bertil, "that giving people money doesn't help them get on their feet, it only fortifies them in their flaw that led them to needing the money in the first place. You might as well take this lesson to heart. I did worse than you though. I gave my money to people who didn't need it and brought out their worst flaws, made those flaws flower. One son is a spendthrift, one a miser, the other a fool. I'm not saying we shouldn't give to the poor. We should. A certain amount of our incomes should go to help others by way of food and housing and education. No one should want. Nor should anyone despoil the landscape building disgusting, big houses like Franz did in order to bury himself in debt."

"Dad, I suppose you are right. I have given money to drunks, gamblers, bigamists, and con men, only to support their habits. I have opened my house to artists, some of whom have no talent at all and don't pull their weight keeping the house running. But these are the people who need money. People of good character generally don't."

Jacob smiled. "You are a wiser man than I and you didn't even get to spend time with the holy man."

"Tell me about him."

Jacob told Bertil about the holy man and then said goodbye. As Jacob walked down the road to the train station, he turned for a last look at his youngest son. Without thinking, he moved to the middle of the road to do so. A car came around the corner and struck him down.

For a week, Jacob was in the hospital with a head injury and a broken leg. Then Bertil, the son who had no money, not to mention no room in his house, took him in to help him recover. One of Bertil's untalented artist friends, a middle-aged woman, nursed him and soon she and Jacob were living as man and wife. When he could walk with a crutch, Jacob took care of the book store while Bertil went on his book-hunting expeditions.

Jacob's months with Anna and the holy man faded to a wonderful dream. He had served his purpose there. He had gone to Ireland to fetch Anna when the holy man needed her, inspired by Ho to do so. He had discovered a good person within his own heart. There was no real reason to return with the holy man gone, his monks disbanded. Anna, no doubt, would go back to Ireland with Errol.

Jacob was glad to be in his own country speaking his own language. He was happy to experience a love relationship and to help out Bertil who had been so kind to him.

One night he awoke suddenly from a dream about Melissa. He remembered the kerchief Melissa gave him saying, 'you don't have to remember us'. He had not forgotten them but the kerchief itself had slipped his mind. In a panic he got up and looked through all his things for the gift the child had given him but it wasn't anywhere. He even awakened his son to ask about it. Bertil said it had been so soaked with blood and dirt they had thrown it away.

Chapter 11
Laughing Woman

Anna was stranded on the mountain. It was well over a month since Jacob had left, almost two months since the others had followed Chen. She couldn't hike the ten miles down to town with the children. It was too far for their little legs. Undoubtedly they would be safe alone in the half-hermitage but she didn't feel right about leaving them. Jimmy, now six, could probably walk the ten miles down and, if they spent the night in town, back up again, but Melissa, almost four, was not up to such a journey and she was too big to carry. Jacob had put enough food in the larder until his return so it wasn't that Anna needed supplies, it was that she was lonely. She was used to having a lot of people around. She had not only lost her beloved

Joe, and Errol, she'd lost everyone. The summer days were long for the children who missed their father. Errol was always up for games and adventures. They missed Kim who had endless ingenious resources for fun and Jacob with his stories, Ho with his music. Again and again Anna heard the plaint, "There's nothing to do," until she wanted to scream. She carved up the hours as best she could: meditation time, cleaning time, playing time, rest, reading, meals, nature walks, so the days passed fully and peacefully but steeped in a pervasive loneliness. She could not even receive her mail which would stay down in the town until she went down or someone came up.

While the children missed Errol's vigor and and madcap sense of adventure, Anna missed his love and the day to day exchange of ideas and feelings and simple comments that married people have. She missed simply having an adult to talk to.

She resigned herself to the fact that possibly no visitors would come up the mountain as long as The Holy Man Is Gone sign stood forbiddingly at the foot of it. Joe had said to put it there so she couldn't take it away. Maybe she could scribble a little addendum: but Anna is here. She smiled at the thought. She was here and she was raring to help life's sufferers. Bring them on.

The mountain was still wet and its long grasses luxuriantly green. Usually by midsummer they had turned to gold. At night she and the children heard frogs singing. By day, they looked but could never find them. One evening after the sun went down, the air was full of bats, although heretofore the mountain had no caves. Maybe it did now. The mountain was full of new tricks and new species.

Then one day, at last, a visitor came. She was a young American, tall and thin, but in good enough shape to carry a huge pack on her back. "Hi, there," she said. "I'm Sally." Anna and the children greeted her and told her their names as she swung the pack off her back, laughing. "I came over-prepared. I'd heard there was a long line and that it would take me a good part of the summer to see the holy man."

"The holy man is gone," said Anna. "Didn't you see the sign at the start of the mountain path."

"No, but maybe the storm took it down. I hear there was a terrible storm a while back. Gosh, I can see it wrecked your habitat here. Where did the holy man go?"

"He died," Jimmy said. "Mom's the holy man now."

The visitor laughed. Whenever Sally laughed, the children laughed, too.

"Joe 'nointed her," Melissa said.

Anna could tell the woman neither knew who Joe was nor what 'nointed meant as she laughed again. And again. Hee, hee, hee - a braying sound.

"What did you want to see the holy man about?" Anna asked, pleased that she was in business and her first customer had finally come. She began to visualize a long line of pilgrims at Sally's heels. "Please sit down." She gestured at all that was left of the patio Kim, Jacob, and Errol had built in the spring, a place where Joe could sit comfortably to greet the pilgrims. Most of the adobe bricks had tumbled down in the storm but the seat Kim had made, fitting rocks together with no cement was still intact and here Anna placed herself on the sun-warmed stones.

Sally, still laughing, sat down. The children had ceased to respond to her laughter which indeed had begun to chafe but they sat down next to her. The natural thing is to join a person in laughter but Sally's laugh was not infectious unless one thought of infectious as making one feel slightly ill. Anna figured the children stayed because they, too, were hungry for a new face. She wondered if it would be all right for them to hear the young woman's problem and decided not to worry about it.

"It will seem like a silly difficulty to come all this way to try and solve. It's my laughing. I can hardly say anything without laughing even when there's nothing funny. It makes me feel like such a jerk." She laughed. "Do you think it's that I want people to like me? I suppose it is a nervous laugh of some sort."

Anna had no idea what to say. At first she tried to think what Joe would say but she didn't feel that was a good way to proceed. She wasn't Joe. She wasn't a seventy three year old holy man. She was a thirty four year old nurse, mother, and protege. A lonely one.

"I can't remember how long this laughing of mine has gone on, when it began or why. It is so much a part of me I hardly notice it but others do. It drives them buggy after a while. As for having boy friends, forget it."

Anna relaxed, realizing she didn't' have to say anything as long as Sally was talking, and the woman seemed to have a lot to say about this laughing of hers. The children were already getting bored and had got up from the bench to resume the checker game they'd been playing with sticks and stones on squares drawn in the dirt.

"I think I was quiet all the way up the mountain, but as soon as I met you I was off laughing once again You tell me the holy man died and I laugh. This is totally inappropriate."

Suddenly the woman started to cry. "It's hopeless."

This is good, Anna thought. She remembered Joe's story of Alim who had climbed the mountain to give Joe a piece of his mind, telling Joe he was a bad thing for the town merchants, spoiling business. Joe of course listened politely. Then Alim had burst into tears and stayed on the mountain for over two years.

Sally's sobbing was rather soothing compared to her laughing. Soon she blew her nose and collected herself. "You sit there so calmly, saying nothing. How do you do it? You have these waves of tranquility radiating from your person." She wiped her eyes and mopped her face. "Whereas look at me." She let loose a laugh that the tears had not diminished.

Finally she grew quiet, neither cried nor laughed nor talked.

Then Anna was inspired to say, "All you need to do is listen."

"Listen?" she repeated, proving she'd done just that.

"Listen to every word and be aware of the person's body language so you're listening to that, too. Gradually you will find that you are responding appropriately. You won't need to laugh and you'll hardly need to talk except when you have something necessary to say, or something nice to say."

"I think I've got it. Yes. I understand. As it is, I don't listen. I only think of what I will say next and how quickly I can intervene with my words, or my laughter. This will take work but it will be worth it. Thank you, Anna. I can't wait to start." She paused. "So speak again so I can practice." She laughed, said, "Oops," and laughed again. "Those laughs don't count because I was making little jokes, right? No? Okay, tell me what to do when people are silent? Although no one is as silent as you, thank God." She clapped a hand over her mouth to stifle another laugh.

"Don't be afraid of wordlessness. Just breathe and think about your breath as it goes in and out. There is never utter silence. Listen to the birds, the grasses moving in the breeze, the sound of air itself, of breath. "Sit here beside me and we will breathe together for a while." They breathed together, listening, and she could almost hear all the knots of Sally's body come untied. After sharing some tea Anna said goodbye, suggesting Sally spend some nights on the mountain on the way down to imbibe of its magic. Anna almost wanted to extend the visit, but she let her go. It was a good moment for her to depart, while she was full of resolve. The only trouble was that since she'd commanded Sally to be a listener, others wouldn't find out about Anna from her, wouldn't learn that she was in business at Joe's place. How could a dedicated listener carry the word of mouth?

Chapter 12
Scavenger

Anna was happy she was in business and that the sign was down. She waited for the next customer but no one came that day or the next or the next. No one else came all summer. Disturbingly, Jacob didn't come either. Every day Jimmy ran a little way down the mountain to meet Jacob but came back bitterly disappointed, mad at both Anna and Melissa for Jacob's failure to come. Periodically one of Alim's children came up with a message from Jacob that he was delayed. Messages also came from Errol that he was designing a sport center for Chen and having a great time. Then the messages from both men stopped.

Finally, after two months, when the summer was practically over, five men appeared at the door.

Four of them were big strong youths who wore baggy shorts with plaid shirts hanging tails out, unbuttoned over dirty white tee shirts. Although the shirts and shorts were different colors, it was like a uniform. Exhausted by the climb, they threw themselves on the ground. Two of them lit cigarettes.

The fifth man appeared to be their leader. He was dressed in long pants, open necked shirt, a wet linen jacket, Panama hat: strange mountain climbing attire, Anna thought. He had sweated through the jacket. He put his arms akimbo and looked around. They had brought a string of the magical mountain ponies with them. The children ran to pet them and hopefully cadge a pony ride. "Are you the care-taker here? We have come for the holy man's things."

She thought by his accent he might be Dutch. He had those crowded teeth the Dutch had. From living in such a crowded country, Joe said once. Because of the teeth, the man's mouth couldn't close properly so he had the look of smiling but it was only a look.

"Did Chen send you?" The words popped out. Since Chen had taken all her monks it seemed natural he would now send people to dismantle the remains of the half-hermitage.

"I came on my own before the locusts descend. The word is out on the internet that the holy man is dead. Anything of his will be worth a fortune at auction."

Anna laughed. "The holy man didn't have any things."

"Look at that beautiful table! Could you boys get it down the mountain? We could put the chairs on the ponies."

"Sure thing." They got onto their feet. "Nothing to it. It's all down hill."

"Downhill can be harder than uphill when the path is tricky," said Anna.

"Shut up. Let us tend to our business."

At this, the children looked shocked.

The table and chairs had been made by some of the earliest monks, bringing the hardwood up from town, board by board. It glowed from the care taken of it over the years by loving hands, the waxing and oiling and polishing.

The children, as they heard the man speak harshly to their mother, came to her side, held on to her robe, and looked at the man solemnly.

"There is a pot by the famous Blackie," said the man, his face lighting up. "I will carry that myself."

It was an oval-shaped vase with a luminous gray glaze that was like the early-morning mountain mist. The monks always put flowers in it, or grasses, and Anna had kept up the tradition. "There isn't much here, is there?" One of the young toughs said to the man.

"It's a hermitage, not a palace," Jimmy said. "Mom, say something," Jimmy implored. "Don't let them do this."

"It's all right, Jimmy."

"Just be quiet and you won't get hurt," they were told. "Stand back."

They took blankets. They took Joe's extra robe, the one he hadn't been buried in. They took any of the plates and mugs that weren't chipped and some of the special chopsticks that Joe had carved with animals on the tops. They cleaned the half-hermitage out.

"You will be better people for having these treasures with you for the little while it will take you to go down the mountain," Anna said. "They are full of the holy man's goodness even though they are just objects."

"These things aren't only going down the mountain, they're going all the way to London and New York City." He seemed proud that he could take them so far and to such important places. "To the great auction houses of the world."

"Good luck," Anna said.

The man didn't know that what he thought were beasts of burden were really the dancing, whirling, fancy ponies of the secret polo-ish game that only war veterans could see. These ponies carried ghostly riders or sometimes, rarely, human ones, but furniture? Anna didn't think so. You might as well ask Bolshoi dancers to pull carts. She would be very surprised if the chairs made it down the mountain except in splinters and even if the five boys carried the table, the boulder-strewn, storm-wrecked, still gushing, path would defeat them. If by chance they made it to the town, good luck getting the holy man's chattels past the townspeople.

Anna shook her head, thinking of the terrible time the laden-down males had ahead of them. When the ponies shunted everything off their backs in one of their pirouettes, the men would pick up the pieces to try to carry themselves, along with everything else they were burdened with and their loads would get beyond heavy. Their loads would crush them. Their hearts would fail them. They would learn that thou shalt not steal. Anna did not need to teach them. The holy mountain would say it all. Poor devils. Anna began to feel sorry for them.

"Goodbye," she waved them away, "Watch your steps."

The children stood by her, very surprised. "Those men are taking our table and chairs. Our blankets. Our everything. There's nothing left."

They ran inside. "Look," said Jimmy, "they forgot the best thing."

On the wall was the official portrait of the holy man.*

"They thought it was only a child's drawing said Melissa, because I was only three when I drew it." This from the height of her four years.

This was the picture Joe had left at Alim's shop to be framed for Anna and given to her upon her return from their journey, knowing he would be dead. "It is the only thing I would have cried to lose," said Anna.

*   *The official picture of the holy man is printed on the last page of The Holy Man's Journey.*

Chapter 13
Turning Suffering to Happiness

Alim came up the mountain the next day. He was a short, sturdy man with greying black hair and mustache and the joined eyebrow typical of the area. His eyes were bright and happy. He had been a workaholic when he first came to Joe but when he left the mountain to return to the town below, he married, had children, relaxed and had fun. His photography store thrived as well as it had in the time when he worked night and day, better, actually, because people liked coming there.

Anna went into the kitchen to make herb tea in the last two (chipped) cups. Alim followed her. "We'll take it outside since there's nothing to sit on here."

Alim smiled and pointed, "There is the picture

of the holy man Joe left with me to be framed when the two of you set off on your journey. He knew he wouldn't return. Wasn't it wonderful he chose Melissa's drawing to be his official portrait. So like him. And so, the scavengers left the most valuable thing, the one thing they could so easily have removed and carried away."

"You saw those men?"

"Oh, yes. They came limping into town with sprained and broken limbs, terrible cuts and bruises, sadder and wiser men than when they went up the mountain. The table is now in my shop and we have gathered the pieces of chairs to put back together. The holy man's robe blew away on a gust of wind. We are still looking for it. We found the blown-away blankets and shall clean them.

"So, Anna, the hermitage table stands alone in my shop because I have retired and removed everything else. Soon the chairs will join it and already Blackie's vase holds flowers on top of it. The shop is there for you and the children to live in during the winter. I was hoping you might come back down to town with me. Before you make your decision, you will want to read these two letters I have from Errol and Jacob. The one from Jacob came two weeks ago." He took his tea outside and left her alone with the letters. "I will talk with the children while you read them."

First she opened Jacob's letter.

"My dear Anna, I have been in the hospital, having been hit by a car. I am afraid my broken leg, although healing, will never take me up the mountain again. My broken head kept me from writing to you until now. Forgive my long silence. I am staying with my sweet, youngest son, helping him in his bookshop. There is a woman I am happy with. I feel at peace. I will not be coming back. You and the children will always be engraved on my heart. Love to you all, your Jacob.

The second letter was from Errol: Dear Anna, this is a very hard letter to write. I have fallen in love with a young woman here at Universe-city and I will not be coming back to the mountain. Chen needs me here. He tells me that through different channels, he has alerted the world to the holy man's demise and no one will be coming to the hermitage. I think you should go home to Ireland with the children where I will come when I can. If possible, we will get an annulment of our marriage, then arrange for custody of the kids. I have to say that Chen makes your holy man look pretty pathetic in comparison. He is a genius, igniting the whole world with his ideas. But the fact is, I guess I have you to thank for meeting him so this lost year away from home hasn't been entirely a wild goose chase. Also, I do miss the mountain. It's pretty flat here and there is a wall all around the city -- a beautiful wall but still a wall and 'something there is that doesn't love a wall' as Robert Frost once said. Jill, my next wife, is a poet. I don't think this letter will come as a big surprise or a big sorrow. Love to the kids, Errol.

Anna tried to hold back tears but to no avail. They burst from her eyes. Her breast heaved. It was a human-sized miniature of the storm that had rearranged the hermitage and mountain. It knocked her to her knees. She howled. All her pent-up loneliness of the summer took part in her bellow of grief and adding to it was her shame for letting go in this unholy way.

"Good, Anna, that is wonderful crying. I'm proud of you. This is a double whammy that deserves such a tempest of grief."

How could she hear Joe's voice through her great wail? It made her stop to hear it better. But there was nothing. Only the small sounds she had preached to the laugher to harken to. While she listened, her crying stopped, turned to hiccups then nothing. Then she remembered the letters and tears sprang to her eyes, her breast heaved, but before she could again release her expression of suffering, she heard, "That's enough, now."

"What? Enough? I've only just got started."

"Oh come on. As Errol said, this news is not a great surprise. Why are you hanging around this broken down hermitage anyhow? Time to be brave and get on with your life. Go on down the mountain with Alim. See what happens next."

Anna went out to find Alim who, unlike Joe, would give her the sympathy she needed. "Alim, my husband has fallen in love with another woman and Jacob, too, has found love. Neither of them are coming back." Saying the pitiful words made her crumple once again, made her age a hundred years.

"Oh, Anna, I can see you are reacting with great hurt, even perhaps with anger. You understand that it is your reaction that is hurting you, not the letters themselves and the words they carry. This is valuable for your practice. Anna, listen. This is a benefit. Because if you can handle this little problem of your husband's and friend's desertions by turning your reaction into happiness and freedom then you will be prepared to take on worse sufferings when they come."

Anna thought Alim sounded more like Joe than Joe.

"Oh, Alim, you remember his teachings better than I."

"Well, of course, it is easy for me since I am not the one who received the horrible letters." Alim laughed.

"Mama, did you say Daddy and Jacob aren't coming home to stay with us," Jimmy asked, running over to her, Melissa hard on his heels.

Anna sank to her knees and put her arms around both children. "Yes, my darlings. They have both found love and happiness where they are."

"That sounds good," said Melissa, dubiously.

"It doesn't sound good," said Jimmy stamping his feet. "I want them to come back right now."

"They'll come visit, won't they?" asked Melissa. Anna said of course but Melissa started to cry and Jimmy, too. Anna joined them and Joe's voice either gave itself a rest or was drowned out by their chorus of sobs. Alim wandered away, feeling a little weepy himself. After a while, Anna called to him, "Alim, we will come down the mountain with you. Thank you for offering your shop. Come on, sweethearts, let's get our things together."

"I bet we will probably take the trail past the ponies?" Alim said.

Tears vanished like magic as the children executed a little dance of pleasure. "You see," Alim gestured toward them. "It is built into the young to anticipate rather than dwell in the present moment, especially when it is particularly abysmal."

"When they were four miles into the ten mile descent, Anna asked Alim why he decided to retire. She was feeling glad that she had decided to turn her sorrow to happiness, her bad, angry, cowardly reaction to a liberating one that allowed her to open herself to the beauty all around. It struck her how the mountain was all in motion: the birds and animals, the grasses, the leaves of trees, the clouds above. And she was in motion, too, despite the downward tugging of her heavy heart. As Joe suggested, she would see what happened next.

"The fact is," Alim replied, "with the holy man gone, there are no more pilgrims, nobody needing cameras, film, and developing. The town has become the little backwater it was when the holy man first arrived."

"Are other businesses suffering?"

"Yes. It is the nature of our people to want to work hard, but we are good at retiring, too. We can get by bartering back and forth with each other. It won't be long until people come to see you, Anna, and then we'll thrive once again."

"I don't know how the word will get out," Anna said. "And if it does, Chen will quash it."

Alim smiled and hugged her affectionately. "If it takes a while to happen, it will only be because you aren't ready. So Chen is aiding you. Giving you time to discover your true holiness. He may intend this or he may not. Whatever, it will be for the good - for you and for us all. Whatever comes to us, in whatever form, is in the long run for the good. Sometimes we have to give it time to have it happen and then to see what has happened."

"Alim, that is just what Joe said."

Alim smiled. He put Melissa on his back and led the way down to the town.

Chapter 14
The Gloomy Jailer

Anna was happy to be living in the town. It was a foothill town of only a few thousand people, stuck somewhere in time around the 1950s with cars of that era mixing it up with vehicles pulled by donkeys, horses, and oxen. It was built on the foothill of the mountain and tumbled down to an agricultural valley. Mountain streams poured through it joining the vaster river below so the town had many stone bridges where the streams cut back and forth on their downward journey. The houses and buildings were mostly of stone and adobe as there were no forests nearby except for a gentle woodland of fragile, flowering and fruiting, trees that bordered the mountain and town and were also planted in the park. The large central park had two stone-sculpted elephants standing on columns at the entrance, a mystery to all since the animal was not of this country. A large fountain played within, surrounded by benches. Acres of mown grass provided playing fields for children, adults, and dogs. Here Joe had come regularly to play with children and Anna resumed his practice.

The narrow, cobbled streets often met in a piazza which contained a church and at least one café – feeling no incongruity in their proximity. In the biggest of these was an open market five days a week where the valley's bounty was displayed and sold. There were the usual public buildings of city hall, library, police station, firehouse, schools, and about twenty stores and shops among which was Alim's now defunct photo shop which sat high on the town's hill at the foot of what had been the Hermitage Trail.

After three months alone on the mountain it was, to Anna, a vast metropolis.

In Alim's shop, she made a cozy home for herself and the children. So many villagers visited, sitting around the hermitage table, that it wasn't long before she had a little tea shop going. The holy man's picture was on the wall. In the center of the table sat Blackie's vase, the color of air, which Jimmy kept full of fresh flowers.

Anna learned to bake the round crusty rolls that were popular with the folk, enhancing them with bits of dried fruit. She served these with the mint and other local herbal teas, the black and green tea that the spice shop imported from Japan and China, and coffee, of course, at least for her. Anna loved her coffee.

To save on dishwashing, each visitor brought their own cup in most cases created by Ezla who was now, as Joe had urged him to become, a potter himself instead of the obsessed pottery collector of former years. Not that he didn't eye Blackie's vase with modified lust every time he came to the tea shop, as Blackie's work had been the thrust of his collection. His cups were often lumpy looking and imperfectly glazed but he kept trying and made a little progress in the craft. Customers washed the cups in a trickle of creek water outside the shop, the gentle dregs of herbs returning to the earth, then hung the cups from lines Anna had strung from the branches of olive trees and on the branches themselves. Ezla cleverly made hooks of the handles so this could be accomplished.

Some paid with the coin of the realm, others brought food from their gardens. In this way, Anna and the children got by. The children picked up the language in no time and, as Anna had been studying it throughout the year, the constant visiting helped her grow fluent.

Each day, six year old Jimmy walked to school, and Melissa went to the park where Anna, as Joe used to do, taught the little children to breathe meditatively and to practice loving kindness to each other. In return, Anna learned from them how to keep herself laughing, joyful, energetic, and innocent – how to maintain the beginner's mind, the ability to see the world afresh.

When the weather allowed, she hiked up the mountain to where she thought the holy man's grave was, and talked to him. She never went back to the hermitage. Coming and going she passed the supernatural dappled ponies and leaned on the rail looking at them as the old warriors: Joe, Jacob and Ho, used to do. She tried to imagine seeing, as the trio had, the ghostly game of polo the dappled ponies played, mounted by townsmen who had died in wars.

Now that she had people to be with whenever she wanted, she cherished her time alone. She thought about her life. Was she fulfilling Joe's hopes for her? She doubted it. She wasn't doing harm, but was she doing any good? She wondered if she should go back to her nursing. She had felt it would distract her from replacing Joe, and doing his work. As well, she had always felt uncomfortable with her gift of healing. Now she was busy with the children and the tea shop after her lost summer on the mountain where she'd been what? Nothing? Maybe she'd been healing from the loss of Joe, the monks, Jacob, Errol. She missed Errol. She missed sex. It was probably unholy of her but the thought of the rest of her life without sex was horrifying. Joining with Errol had been their happiest times together, a prologue to their most intimate talks. They'd had a rule of never going to sleep with any trouble between them, to talk it out, to love it out, and they always had. Until Anna had joined the holy man and Errol's unhappiness had turned inward where it couldn't be reached to talk about.

Secretly Anna wondered if she wasn't a little crazy from Joe dying and everyone leaving her never to return, crazy to remain in this foreign land where she and her children were the only ones with red hair? Why was she still here? If she was waiting, what was she waiting for? One realization had been borne in upon her these last months and finally accepted: that she was not a holy woman, anointed or not. She was not now, not before or, which was hardest to accept, not to become, the holy person to replace Joe. She was only holy in the sense everyone was. Still, she promised herself, there was no reason she couldn't be a first rate tea shop proprietor and make that her gift to humanity, or at least to the townspeople.

One day, toward dusk, the sky a pinkish blue, an autumn breeze riffling through the drying leaves, causing some to set sail in the lavender air, a man joined her as she leaned on the fence watching the ponies.

"Can you see the game?" she asked him. His face was vivid with the typical joined eyebrows, round dark eyes, and jutting chin of the villager. His body was short and ropy, his legs a little bowed.

"Yes, I've drawn blood in my day and been bloodied in return," he said gloomily.

His gloomy tone reminded her of Jacob. She experienced a pang in her heart, missing him so much. Also the fellow's earthy smell, just shy of being a stink, reminded her of Errol when he'd been working hard. She missed him, too, but not in the way she missed Jacob. Thanks to Alim's view of her trouble, she had not nursed any anger or resentment towards Errol but there was definitely a wound, a sore place, a tenderness in her psyche from his desertion.

"You're the holy woman, then?"

"I guess."

"I hear everyone left you stranded." He said this with some relish as if she deserved it, as if any woman did, holy or not.

"Yes. I'm the stranded holy woman."

"I'm the town jailer. You wouldn't press charges on the men who came and took the holy man's things from the hermitage. What an idiot. Why not? They deserved punishment."

"They were just things."

"Give me an idea what you would put someone in jail for?"

"It isn't up to me, thank goodness. I believe there have to be laws, but I'm glad I'm not in charge of them. Everyone is a holy person. They just have to find out."

"If you could see some of my prisoners, you'd change your mind. Sewer rats. Jail's too good for them."

"Then I will come to the jail and see them."

After that, Anna went once a week to the jail, bringing fresh rolls and It's Good Luck to be Nice kerchiefs, the message mostly obscured by the pattern so they could notice it or not. For some reason there were a lot of the kerchiefs left and she wanted to give the prisoners something to make an excuse for her visits. (Jimmy eventually told her there were a lot left because the three disabled woman kept making them and replenishing the pile).

Anna suffered obscene remarks and ugly looks from some of the prisoners but persisted in her visits and was in due course rewarded by welcoming smiles and small presents in return that they fashioned from bits of wood, string, cloth, and beads that their families brought to them. At the tea shop Anna had a special shelf for her prison art. The gloomy jailer began to like his job. He gave her a present, too. He carved a pirouetting dappled pony that had all the grace and jauntiness of the real thing. He gave it to her, saying, "You can't see the rider, but he's there."

"You couldn't see the holiness in your prisoners, but it was there."

"Nah! It's you transformed them with your own stranded holiness."

"No, it's their own, I promise you, as yours is your own. Thank you for the lovely carving."

Chapter 15
Dogs

One day, Melissa came home from her nearby play school with a huge, shaggy, brown dog with stand-up ears and a flat, wrinkled face. He and the child were both covered with snow. The little girl smiled, throwing an arm over the dog's neck which was as high as her head. The dog licked her face and she giggled. "Momma, this is Bear. He's abandoned, like us."

"We're not abandoned."

"Everyone left us, didn't they? When are Daddy and Jacob coming to see us?" This used to be a daily question, but came less and less as time went by.

"We can't feed such a huge dog. Anyhow, we're vegetarians."

"He doesn't care. He needs a family to love and protect. Dogs are people, too, you know."

Bear went to the fireplace and lay down, looking at Anna with almost the same mournful look as the gloomy jailer. "Make yourself at home," Anna said. "Want some tea?"

Melissa laughed. Jimmy came home, took off his jacket and sat down on the floor by the dog, patting him. "Can we keep him?"

"If he'll eat rice."

"We can get bones from the butcher."

"No we can't. We don't believe in killing animals. Or anything."

"Not even an ant," said Melissa. "But if Bear wants to chew a bone we didn't give him, that's okay, isn't it?"

"That's called turning a blind eye to something that is wrong. It's bad action, almost worse than approving the wrong."

"Approving?" Melissa stumbled over the word.

"Telling yourself it's all right."

"But it's natural for a dog to eat meat and they don't kill for it," said Jimmy. "He just accepts it nicely from the butcher after the butcher has told him to 'Sit'."

"We're not bringing bloody gristly bones into our house. He can get enough protein from nuts and cheese that we'll mix in with his rice."

"Oh goody, we can keep him," Melissa said.

"Do you understand about the blind eye?" Anna persisted with her lesson.

"It's pretending you didn't see something," Jimmy said. "Something bad. Something you could have done something about when you saw it. If you were a grown-up."

"When those men came and took our things from the hermitage and you let them, were you turning blind?" Melissa asked.

"No. I didn't care about those things. And I knew I was helpless to do anything about it. It would have been a different story if they wanted to take you, my darling."

"But wouldn't you still have been helpless?" Jimmy asked.

"No, I would have fought with the strength of ten."

"Or you could have turned them nice, like everyone says you've done with the prisoners."

"I certainly would have tried that first." Anna smiled and kissed her children.

Jimmy persisted with his lesson, "If Bear gets

his own meat and we don't know about it, that's okay, right?"

"But then he might want to go live with the meat people," Melissa worried.

"We might want to, too," said Jimmy, eyeing his mother.

"Yes," Anna said. "One day, no doubt, you're going to want to have hamburgers."

What are hamburgers, they wondered.

Later, when the children were in bed she said, "Well, Bear, I've learned something today. Dogs are people, too."

Chapter 16
Birds

Meanwhile, in the glitter, spangle, and grandeur of the Universe-city, which was well into and beyond the year 2001, Joe's monks were finding it was not a pleasing place to be. It wasn't just Chen's fleet of fancy cars, his bodyguards, his isolation from his followers, the fact that they bowed to him but he didn't to them, it was that after the first thrill was gone, they felt empty being there, almost despairing. It was a place of delusion. Chen's teachings were brilliant. He was charismatic and beautiful. But there was no soul, no love, no peace. One by one they left and returned to their fruitful lives.

Errol remained. For him the thrill was daily more thrilling as he worked with other designers and builders on the new sport's center, leading the team, finding it intellectually and esthetically challenging. The night was thrilling, too, as he lay with his young bride-to-be, awhirl in the infatuation of new love and inflated with her adoration of him.

The strange thing was that, although he never thought of Anna, except occasionally with alienation, and only sometimes of the children, he often thought of Joe. Joe's face would appear in his mind's eye at the oddest times - gentle, smiling, understanding. Errol remembered the night he'd come in to the hermitage, half frozen from being caught in a storm, and Joe had hot soup for him as well as some strong words about his behavior. They'd bonded then. What would Joe think of his behavior now? And yet, Joe's features did not contain any accusation, only that infernal understanding. It annoyed the hell out of him.

He talked to Chen about it. Chen replied, "Yes, it is terrible to be so completely understood. It's what we all yearn for, to be understood and forgiven, but it's hard to handle. We want to be seen as the front we've fabricated. Joe never would pay attention to a man's front no matter how carefully the man had erected it to withstand the toll of the years of his behavior and the penetration of his observers."

"Why is he looking at me from the grave. I don't feel in the least guilty if that's what he wants."

"Oh, Joe never tried to make a man feel guilty. He just wanted us to ..."

"To?"

"To know ourselves, to recognize that there was a false front and remember what was behind it. To remember the little boy who grew into Errol, to get back inside that child and see through his eyes."

"I was an angry little boy."

"Which is why you were drawn to anger-less Anna and why you came to resent her for her lovingness, feeling that if she couldn't see things as you saw them, she was deluded about life."

"That's right! Don't you think she's deluded?"

"No." Chen accepted a glass of liquid that was presented to him on a silver plate. When he touched the plate Errol wondered why a strange shiver ran over his features. Whatever it was, Chen shrugged it away, saying, "Now, let's have a look at those plans."

Errol unrolled the papers.

After a half hour of Chen's critique, from which Errol learned a great deal, Errol said enthusiastically, "Let's plant trees. You have your parks of intricate waterways, fountains and pools, but no trees. If we plant them, the birds will come. There are no birds here."

"There are no birds because I don't like droppings."

"But surely you don't kill them?"

Chen laughed. "No. The birds know not to come."

The birds know not to come. Errol found the words frightening. For the first time he had a feeling of wanting to leave. But Jill had another year of her education and it would be more than a year to complete the sport's center and derive the notoriety of it appearing in all the architectural digests and magazines as Chen's other building's had. He couldn't relinquish his coming fame or his new love. He forgot his fear and instead felt more fascinated by the power of this man who could create this wondrous city, have thousands of ardent followers and, on top of all that, tell the birds where not to fly.

Chapter 17
Smiling Man

The holy man had never written down his teachings. He felt they were fluid, always changing, that he himself was busy learning. He didn't want his thoughts and ideas frozen in time. He didn't want to be 'stopped in his tracks'. But Jacob, during his convalescence, thought it wouldn't hurt to write down some little stories about the time he had spent with the holy man, not as a monk, since he wasn't one, but as sort of the holy hanger-on. This way he could perpetuate the memory of the holy man. He published the little volume privately and whenever he sold a book at his son's store, he slipped it in with the purchase. After writing to Anna about his inability to return, he got a letter from her applauding his decision, sending all her love, and also a new kerchief: "since yours might have got lost in the accident". She said everything was fine but Jacob heard from friends in the town about Errol's non-return (along with his own), about the scavengers trying to clean her out, about her being alone with the children on the mountain in the half-hermitage all summer.

He would have tried to go but the pins that had been put in his leg created infections and in the end his leg was lost to gangrene. He was a tough old man who never complained, who felt grateful for being alive at all. Writing his little book was a healing experience in itself. He continued to slip it into purchaser's bags, one of whom, one day, was a man who looked like he was smiling so that Jacob smiled back, but it turned out he wasn't – he simply couldn't get his lips over his teeth.

"My name is Lootjens. I am a book collector from The Netherlands. This is a nice little book of yours. I think it might become a collector's item in due course when a publisher picks it up. I'd like to buy about fifty of them."

"Have you read it?" Joe had dealt enough with collectors to know that they often weren't readers.

"Of course."

"Tell me the names of Joe's monks."

"What? Am I to be tested?"

"It's not for sale," said the holy hanger-on. "I want people to read it. I don't want fifty copies gathering dust in your apartment."

The man offered Jacob large sums of money, which Jacob considered accepting to send on to Anna, but he said no. Lootjens offered to find a publisher for the book in return for the fifty copies, and Jacob thought about how that would catapult the stories into the hands of many readers, but he didn't like this man so he said no. The book would find its own way.

He thought of saying, "Save the money and fix your teeth," but he didn't think the holy man would approve of what he would perceive as a wise remark, a smart remark. Funny how mean-edged remarks were termed smart and wise when they were neither in the real sense of the word .

"This holy man never let anyone take his picture, never wrote down his teachings," Lootjens explained. "At this point in time, I believe I am the only man trying to collect any ephemera having to do with him."

"I wonder if you were the man who went to his hermitage to steal his possessions."

"I am!" The man looked proud. "Not to steal. To collect. I climbed the mountain."

"As thousands did before you."

"But there is no path now. I guarantee it was a feat."

For collectors, the thrill of the hunt was part of their obsession. They liked to imagine dangers involved.

"However, for one reason or another," he said vaguely, "everything was lost." He spread his arms to signify the odd disappearance but Jacob knew the real story and knew a lying bastard when he saw one.

Jacob commented wryly. "When people tried sneakily to photograph the holy man, to steal his image that is, there was never an image when they developed the pictures."

"How strange." Lootjens laughed an outstandingly fake laugh. "Maybe I have not read your book because there is no print in it," accusing Jacob now of stealing the holy man's words. Oh, he was quick, Jacob thought. Quick and slick.

"I'm surprised you weren't arrested for trying to take Joe's things."

"The woman, the little caretaker or whatever she was, did not press charges." Again he looked proud. He had gotten away with something. "She let me take his things without a word. No, not true.

As I was leaving, she said. 'Good luck. Watch your step.'"

Jacob's heart was wrenched to think of Anna being there when this man and his thugs appeared. For the first time in many years he desired to, not exactly murder a man, but to hurt him very badly. Jacob had to put his hands behind his back so they would behave themselves and not act involuntarily. His hands had been very quick in their day, faster than the speed of thought.

"But I had very bad luck indeed," the man continued blithely. He elaborated on the wind taking some of the things, other items breaking when the men fell down. He told how the horses bucked off the chairs and dishes that were tied on their backs and then galloped away.

Jacob was enchanted to hear it.

"The vase I carried remained intact but was taken from me by one of the villagers."

"So you are left with nothing."

"Nothing. I am thinking to return for some of the holy rubble of his hermitage Properly managed, I could sell pieces of it. But what a trip! Why not save myself the trouble and create my own rubble."

"Yes, forged rubble," said Jacob. "Why not?"

Lootjens laughed. He was the kind of man who did not have a natural laugh in him so had taught himself to make the sound of a laugh, had learned to take his cues that someone had made a joke. To accentuate his faux laughter, he clapped his hands at the same time, not with elbows bent but with long arms so that he clapped in front of his genitals.

This man has holiness in him, Jacob reminded himself of Joe's teaching, but he was getting depressed talking to him. "Goodbye," he said and turned abruptly away, bringing his aching hands with him, so that those wily appendages of his would continue to behave and not lash out with any of their assassin's tricks that were wired into his system from long ago.

Chapter 18
Seeing Joe

It was spring in the town and Jimmy and Melissa were out Creek Stomping, an annual event for the town's children. This meant they put on boots and went walking through the creek around the town, under bridges. It was watery and marvelously muddy but only a few inches deep. They only had a few days to do so before the snow-melt came coursing down and made the creek too dangerous -- although that was when the older kids got into hand-made boats and let it take them to the valley. Later still, with rain and more snow melt, they wouldn't make it under the bridges without getting bonked on the head. As it was, the cascades and waterfalls left a lot of walking-wounded teenagers.

Melissa was young for creek-stomping but

Anna figured with Jimmy and Bear beside her she'd be safe. The worst that could happen would be she would get too tired but she was strong for a little girl turning five this summer. As it was, Jimmy came home without her. No Melissa.

"Where is Melissa? You promised me you'd take care of your little sister."

Anna listened to her aggrieved tone and thought how unholy it was, how un-Joe. Yet, down through the centuries, it was the tone mothers had taken to their children when they were bad. And what was holier than being a mother and doing the hardest, most important, most self-sacrificing job in the world: nurse, teacher, cook, cleaner, beneficent dictator -- it encompassed a lot of qualities for one person to shoulder and that magnificent person was usually a woman.

"Jimmy, you were supposed to wait up for her if she lagged behind."

"But she didn't," Jimmy protested with all the outraged innocence at his command, his eyes alight in his mud-splattered face. "She and Bear got ahead of me and when I came around the corner she was nowhere."

"Because you'd probably stopped to throw stones and build dams," Anna said.

Jimmy hung his head.

"I asked you to be responsible for your little sister."

"She's okay. There's kids everywhere. And Bear is with her."

"Bear could go chasing after a rabbit and forget about her. What would Melissa do then?"

"Bear's a vegetarian."

"He chases for fun. Dogs are children, too. Now go and clean up. I'm going down to the creek to give a shout."

Anna fretted an hour away, venturing short ways in all directions for some sight of her little girl, querying passers-by, shouting up and down the creek, then running home to see if she had returned.

The creek was safe, she told herself, and it was a nice town where everyone looked out for the children, but the town had a jail for a reason and strangers did come through. She decided to organize a search. It was starting to rain and it would soon be dark. She went home to make calls. Once inside, Bear scratched at the door and pushed it open. He was soaking wet. "Jimmy, here's Bear. Get the towel and wipe him down. Oh, Bear, now I'm really worried. Where's Melissa?"

Bear looked back through the open door. Anna ran out and saw Melissa down the street, wet and bedraggled, walking very slowly, pulling what seemed to be a big pile of rags.

"Oh, Melissa, sweetheart!" Anna ran and embraced her, squatting down to her level. "I've been so worried. Are you all right?"

"I've brought you the most wonderful thing," Melissa said, her teeth and eyes shining through the mud. "Can you take it the rest of the way?"

Anna looked dubiously at the mound of slimy cloth tangled in sticks and stones. Wonderful indeed, thought Anna, wonderfully hideous. She didn't express her disgust for the object but took over dragging it home. It was extremely heavy and she could not imagine why the little child had forced herself to lug it the whole way or how she had managed. What did Melissa think she had here?

"You'll see, you'll see. It's a present."

"We'll just leave it outside for now," Anna said when they were back at the tea shop. I don't think anyone will take it." Ugh, she thought to herself.

Despite all the little girl's effort, she seemed to forget about the present she had worked so hard to bring to her mother. After her bath, her supper, it was early to bed and fast asleep. Jimmy followed soon after. Anna forgot the present, too. It rained in the night, starting with a meek pitter-patter then augmenting to a steady fall. She didn't hear the tiny clatter of stones and sticks separate themselves from the filthy tumbleweed of cloth as it uncoiled in the rain. When she awoke to a yellow dawn and perceived that the dripping sounds were just from the eaves and leaves, no longer the sky, she opened the door to the new day, and saw that Melissa's bundle had dissolved in the night. The debris had come loose, the mud and dirt had washed away and there at her doorstep was the holy man's robe, the color of the sun-risen sky, the robe the Dutchman had taken from the hermitage, the robe which had blown away during his calamitous descent of the mountain.

Somehow it was is if Joe himself had come to her door.

Anna took it in, washed it with soap and water and hung it to dry. It was torn almost to pieces and the pieces were worn through in places as if ground away. It was barely sewn together, more of a piece of cloth than a robe, more gauze than cloth.

When Melissa came in for her breakfast porridge she showed no surprise at seeing the robe hanging there.

"How did you know it was Joe's robe?" Anna asked.

"It smelled like Joe."

"You mean, smelled of the mountain, the earth, the flowers ...?"

"I just knew it was Joe," Melissa said with her captivating little shrug.

Anna let it hang there for some days and loved its presence but she knew Joe would abhor the idea of his robe becoming a relic and remembered his story of how one set of monks' robes had eventually become rags, useful to the end.

She would make pillows of it for her and the children's beds. She used new cloth as backing and decided to embroider on the weary robe-cloth to help hold it together. She stitched the outline of the hermitage as it had been before the storm and then embroidered the words Joe would reply to the pilgrims as they were led out the door. They would complain to Joe, thinking he was a servant. They couldn't leave yet. They had come to see the holy man. Joe would smile and say, You have seen me.

Chapter 19
Thief

"Mom, where's Blackie's vase?" Jimmy asked, his hands full of flowers a villager had brought to them.

"Why, isn't it on the table?" Anna came out of the kitchen where she'd been baking. She glanced around the room. Although colorless, the vase always shone like a candle.

"Do you think someone took it?" Jimmy asked.

"I certainly do not."

"That Dutchman took it once. Maybe he sneaked back."

"I know what, Jimmy. I think Ezla has it. He thought he saw a little crack or blemish in it that he wanted to fix. It will be back soon. Meanwhile, put the flowers in some cups."

Anna went to the door and gazed out over the town. "Oh, Ezla!" she whispered softly.

Ezla, in his house near the town square, took the vase from under his jacket and set it on a table where the light was best. For five minutes he exulted in its possession. Now, as far as he knew, he had all the extant Blackie pots.

A year ago, Ezla had taxied the holy man and Anna to the airport and asked Joe advice about his collecting mania. Joe had adjured him to make his own pots, discover the joy of creation rather than the lust to possess.

"But Joe," he said now, aloud, presenting his defense. "My creations are terrible. As soon as I take in hand a pile of clay I become Mr. Fumble Fingers. I know. I know. I haven't been at it long, but a little child comes to my studio for the first time and makes a pot that puts mine to shame. Yes, yes, I enjoy having the child come and helping her to make the little ashtray for her father or the bowl for her mother. Yes, that is all very nice, but don't you see that by collecting Blackie's pots I have preserved them from harm. I don't think you understood that part, Joe. They are not for me, they are for posterity. For a museum. Right,

I know, stop, yes, I was going to take a room of my house to be Blackie's museum so people could come to see them and I will, I will, I can't do everything at once.

"Don't you remember …? Oh, right, you were dead by then, when the Dutchman came and took Blackie's vase. Why, that could happen again. I am saving the vase from vile men such as he and … such as me? Oh, please, please, don't league me with such a despicable creature who tried to take everything he could get his polluted hands on and only took Blackie's vase because there were so few things else of Joe's. He had no discernment, no taste, no eye for beauty as I do. He was a plundering thug. I am a man of … Yes, I am a thief. All right. Yes I am. And I have stolen from dearest, kindest Anna who has sent all her customers to me for their tea cups. So, by taking the vase (which, by the way has completely lost is glow since you have enlisted it in teaching me this lesson) I cannot any longer, ever again, go back to Anna's profound and sublime tea shop and sit at the table previously adorned by its ray of beauty, the vase, stolen by me, her family friend. I have effectually banned myself from her company and that of the townspeople just so I can in secret look at this vase which I can hardly see now it's grown so dim.

"Okay, I'm taking it back now, now before they will even know it's missing, before it grows so dim and dull it disappears entirely and yes, I will open the museum and yes, I will keep working at my potting and glazing and maybe in ten years Mr. Fumble Fingers will no longer create poor, paltry, misbegotten pots but will take from the fire one day a pot worthy of Blackie's Museum."

"Mom, Mom, Ezla's already back with the pot. He's fixed it already."

"Thanks, Ezla," Anna called from the kitchen.

Chapter 20
Seeing The Hermitage

The day came when the ebullience of spring with its rushing waters, falling rain showers, and gusty winds, had calmed down enough for Anna to feel she could attempt the climb up the mountain to see how the hermitage had survived the winter. Maybe there was a sneaky part of her heart or mind telling her that she could try to spend another summer up there and see if anyone came. Maybe there was a little glittering residue within that said she was still a once and future holy woman.

Oh, it was wonderful to be on the mountain again. She felt strong and limber. Even on the steep trail, or non-trail, she was making about three miles an hour. She had told the children she might spend the night and they were provided for. Every part of the climb had memories for her, but Anna was one who lived wholly in the present. She knew she wouldn't view the hermitage until she was almost at the doorstep, but as she approached, she could swear there was a shimmering light beckoning her forward. She had a crazy thought that someone was there in advance of her and had set up floodlights to take pictures.

When she arrived, the sight that awaited her was so unexpected that she couldn't integrate it at first. It was the hermitage, and yet it wasn't the hermitage. It was a ruin. There were still skeletal remains that gave it height and shape but it was a ruin, a place that seemingly had not been lived in for years, for centuries. It was wholly entwined with flowers and leaves in a way that would take more than one spring to accomplish for the vines were thick and impenetrable. And thorny. For, along with wild morning glories and trumpet flowers was a wildly clambering rose that heretofore she had seen only down near the town. Here was an ancient, hallowed place. And it shone. A light emanated around it although Anna could not for the life of her determine its source. It was so beautiful, so blessed, that Anna found tears were streaming down her face. She walked around and around, studying the structure. It combined the patriarchal sturdiness of a timeless ruin with the insubstantial feeling of a vision. It wavered before her eyes. Was it the shining that caused that effect? Or was it the motion of its flowers and leaves in the light breeze, the reverberations set up by the wriggling, scuffling, and fluttering of small animals, birds, and lizards? Was it the sun from above combining with the light from within? Or was it all of this that gave Anna to feel it was a wraith of a ruin, a dream, a molecular dance.

Whatever it was, it was not to be inhabited ever again. Not only was the holy man gone, but the sign below should also read that the hermitage, too, was gone. In its place was a shrine, a sainted ruin, but one that must remain secret because Joe deplored such ideas. He wanted people the world over to live lives of loving kindness, of respect for each other, of truthfulness and usefulness, but he never wanted to be worshiped or have any articles of his be adored. Of the thousands who had come to see him, most of them never even knew that they had seen him, until afterward, when they carried his message away.

Anna spent the night to see if the hermitage would shine in the dark but it did not. The stars shone around it. It was only a dark splotch in front of the stars. It was the non-shining, that convinced her the ruin was still there.

A year ago the monks had tried to convince her not to try to carry on Joe's work on her own. The mountain has spoken, they said. Now, the hermitage had spoken. Go back to your tea shop. That is where you belong.

Early the next morning she took the non-trail down from the non-hermitage. Her customers would be looking for her. She had work to do.

As she approached the shop and saw the lines on the olive tree branches strewn with bright ceramic colors like Christmas decorations she thought, "Wow, what a lot of cups. I never noticed because I was always inside. Business is booming."

Chapter 21
Seeing Anna

Business was booming. The tea shop had become a meeting place among the townspeople of all ages, a resting place, a chess-playing place. The cups proliferated on the branches of the trees while folding tables and chairs had appeared and were scattered in the yard for those that wished to sit outdoors. The children and their friends helped serve the buns and the customers carried the hot pots of tea and coffee from the kitchen to pour into cups. Money appeared in payment as well as barters.

Anna, mostly in the kitchen baking, or talking to whoever came in for more tea, coffee, or buns, rarely went out into the actual shop, and so wasn't aware of its new popularity or, if she was, put it down to its being summer, with all the children out of school. The townspeople were always a noisy group so the din was about the same. She didn't notice how the din diminished when she did appear in the shop, how the citizens stopped talking to smile at her, or greet her shyly, didn't notice how they almost held their breath to see who she would touch, for she had a way of approaching one of them from behind, laying her hands on his or her shoulders, then sending fluttering fingers to run through the hair like a wafting of air, and how the others would see the chosen one pervaded with ease, face glowing, eyes bright with moisture. It was the same way she had touched her own children ten thousand times, without even thinking about it. She greeted everyone by name, made casual inquiry regarding their families or selves and smiled a welcome to any strangers.

At first she didn't notice there were a handful of Europeans, now, or Americans, Great Britons, folks from all over once again in the town.

She didn't hear conversations such as this one between foreigner and villagers whose combined English kept the conversation afloat. "I heard about the holy man's death, the storm, and how the hermitage was destroyed."

"Yes, yes, all true."

"We've been up on the mountain of course. Nothing there. Well, nothing but the views and the splendor."

"We call the holy man's mountain a magic mountain. Joe would be glad you went up there."

"Joe? You called him Joe?"

"Sure. That was his name."

"Tell me this. Didn't he choose one of his monks to replace him?"

The villagers shrugged and shook their heads. "Could be, "said one. "Such a thing is possible. Who knows?"

"Well Anna might know, of course," said another. "She was one of his monks. Anna, whose tea shop this is."

"You mean, the pretty young woman who was just out here?"

"Yes, Anna."

"It is said that the chosen one was a woman. I imagined an old woman of course. It couldn't be this Anna. Could I see her, talk to her, ask her?"

"Oh, no. She is very busy."

"But what if by some amazing chance she is the holy woman I've come to see?"

"Why, then, you are very lucky."

"Why is that?"

"Because you have seen her."

Chapter 22
Rubble Rumblings

The Dutchman did not let go of his idea to collect the rubble of the holy man's hermitage and as spring, then summer, came to his frozen country he was filled with optimism. This time he would approach the hermitage with careful planning. For one thing he had an idea to take the bookstore Austrian with him. That man, Jacob, knew Anna and knew the people of the town and would arrange easy access for him and his team. They would be treated with respect this time. Not that the little woman hadn't treated him with respect. She had and, come to think of it, it was a small bit amazing considering the circumstances. But oh, yes, now he understood (for he had finally read Jacob's book as part of his careful planning) the Holy Man's teaching was to treat everyone as a holy man and the little woman was following this demented creed to the letter. Imagine such a thing! And Jacob, having subscribed to the teaching, must also have considered him, Lootjens, a holy man. A striking idea and one that could certainly benefit him. So, he would go to Jacob and propose the trip, offering him a handsome reward to accompany him if he would appease everyone in his path both going up the mountain and when coming down fully laden although, considering the weight of rubble, he wondered if helicoptering the prize directly to the airport would not be well worth the expense. The little woman, ostensibly the holy man's successor, would certify that the rubble was indeed from the hermitage and Jacob would assist him there, also, since, according to his pamphlet, Jacob and Anna were like father and daughter.

Lootjens had prepared a market analysis, testing various auction houses, for the sort of price he might safely ask for the holy rubble and the results were promising. The holy man's reputation was burgeoning throughout the world. If he could somehow throw in some sort of miracle attached to the rubble - all the better. The Dutchman rubbed his hands together and let loose his bark of a laugh, even though no one had made even a semblance of a joke, least of all him.

Oh the joy of putting things over on people and making money at the same time, he thought, looking around his joyless house where he breathed the stale air of his joyless life. Spasmodically he crumpled Jacob's pamphlet into his fist. People are such fools, he thought, such fools. Let them go out into the real world and see how many holy people there are, how many treating others as if they were holy. What kind of world would that be, eh? Eh?

Chapter 23
More Rubble Rumblings

In another less-frozen part of the world, high desert, Chen also had rubble on his mind. Chen, the wise, the beautiful, the immaculate, and, he believed, the immortal, had developed a fascinating and hideous flaw. Everything he touched turned to dross. If he touched silver, it turned to lead. Walking on his Persian carpets, he left a trail of worn and faded colors. His treasured automobile collection was looking increasingly shabby despite the care his pupils took to restore their purring engines and glossy finishes after each outing.

Joe had told him he must let in birth, death, even sickness to his city, that it should not be a place only for the young and preternaturally healthy. He had died to prove his point. But Chen's philosophy of immortality was predicated on the consciousness training of the selected ones who matriculated at his Universe-city. Babies, the sick, the old, had no place here. He sincerely meant to do as Joe had showed him he must. He knew Joe had tried to put his heart in the right place but time passed and things remained the same. He could not bring himself to turn everything upside down to make the change Joe required of him. Now, perhaps as a result, all he touched turned to ugly. No matter that no one else saw the damage his touch presented - he saw it.

He remembered the five days he spent at the hermitage when he had brought back Joe's body. He felt purified there, recharged. He had already been electrified by Joe's death. At that time, while within the hermitage walls, his Midas touch was still extant. Thinking of those five days, he saw a way to circumvent this birth-sickness-death issue and keep the exalted construct of his own beliefs - that one need not get sick and die, therefore there was no need for birth.

He was not the first to think this. The Taoist wise men lived for hundreds of years. The Judaic Christian bible recounted equally long lives. Chen had trained himself to live in the eclipse of time, to extend forever the moment athletes, artists, and lovers discover and inhabit when time stands still, the zone.

He felt he would be healed of this maddening flaw if he brought Joe's hermitage walls to his own house. He would incorporate them into his own living quarters, then his touch would once again make everything blossom, the animate as well as the inanimate.

Errol, his architect, the husband of the sublime Anna, had stayed on even after Joe's monks who had attended him here had left in disgust. Being compassionate men, their disgust was not apparent, but Chen understood that, as followers of Joe, Chen's chosen existence was anathema to them. They weren't palace kind of guys.

Errol, his resident architect, was not a convert to his ideas as yet, but he was a talented, intelligent man whom Chen enjoyed having by his side. He was a hard worker and the perfect choice to put his new plan in motion.

"I want you to return to Joe's mountain and collect the remains of Joe's hermitage," he told Errol, who's jaw promptly fell with astonishment. "Never mind the stone foundation or the supporting wooden beams. I want the walls Joe touched and leaned on, the floors he trod."

"But, Chen, the hermitage is all demolished by the storm, remember? It is mostly rubble except for the one room where Anna and the children still live."

Errol seemed to wake from a dream and realize it was the end of spring, that Anna could not possibly have remained on the mountain through the winter. The year had flown by. He was completely out of touch with his family.

"Exactly. That is what I want - the rubble. The holy man's rubble is for you to insinuate into my own walls."

Errol continued to look astonished which pleased Chen.

"Even if I could undertake this insurmountable task ..."

"Hardly insurmountable. Whole castles have been transferred from one country to another and rebuilt stone by stone."

"Nevertheless, it is Anna's dwelling place."

"No longer. She lives in the town now."

"She does? Still ... I would have to ... go begging to her. She is the custodian. I am hardly in a position to ..."

"You are above begging?"

"I virtually abandoned her. I haven't sent her any money. Of course I've yet to be paid." Errol quickly back-pedaled from what might be heard as a complaint. "Not that I'm not incredibly grateful to live here, to do the job. But, give me a break! Think of my having to ask any favor of Anna."

"Yes, you left her and the children impoverished and alone."

"She had Jacob," Errol said quickly, defensively.

"I'm afraid not. He also left her never to return. She has taken a lowly job in the town to make ends meet, to feed your children and herself."

Errol flushed. "How do you know all this?"

"There is nothing easier than gathering information - if one is curious. But enough of Anna. It is not one's circumstances that determine contentment, it is ones reaction to circumstances. One's temperament, or how one has trained the brain to deal with difficulties. Anna would never feel mistreated, wronged, or even forlorn. I assure you she prospers spiritually."

"But ..."

"Prepare to go in a month's time. You will take my private jet and there will be a helicopter available at the airport for your use after you have reconnoitered and discussed things with Anna. Errol, you are equal to the task. And a little begging will do you a world of good."

"Wait. Your city's architecture is all steel, glass, marble, titanium. How am I to integrate adobe successfully, the humblest of materials."

"That is part of the task."

Chen saw Errol depart with his jaw still slightly hanging. It was good to give the man a creative jolt as well as to emotionally perturb him. For an unspiritual person, not in training, the Universe-city can be a paradise, and therefore demolishing to character. But Chen didn't care about Errol, he cared about Anna which is why he had taken Errol away from her. It had been something of a shock to Chen (except that Chen didn't shock) when Jacob abandoned her, too. That hadn't been part of his orchestration. It was like composing a symphony with stringed instruments abounding and on the night of its debut finding the stage set with piano, percussion and brass. Chen suspected that maybe it made a better symphony.

Chapter 24
Pride

"I have to tell you this is a marvelous little book," Lootjens said to Jacob as he entered the book store, shaking the rain from his umbrella and setting it by the door. "Short as it is, I have spent many hours with it pondering its philosophy of life which you have so charmingly presented."

"Well, thank you for that," said Jacob, surprised to find the color coming to his cheeks. Because it was his habit to slip the anonymous holy man book into the bags of book purchasers, he never had any response. In a long life given to being a warrior, then a business man, then a holy bodyguard to Joe and Anna, and now a clerk in a country bookstore, his writing of the book was his only creative endeavor. He had struggled to put into words his experiences with Joe and struggled hard to keep it simple and easy to read. He was pleased with Lootjens' words, even delighted. He had misjudged the man at their first meeting or, not impossibly, Lootjens' character had altered just from reading the book. Wouldn't that be something if, everywhere, people were changing because of his book just as they had changed from seeing Joe himself.

He found himself offering Lootjens a coffee then another with a little splash of cognac. The two men talked cosily while the rain battered the roof. Jacob, monosyllabic at the best of times, found himself sharing reminiscences with the Dutchman about his time with Joe and Anna, and suddenly felt a longing to return to the site of his happiness. It was natural for Jacob, then, when Lootjens proposed the journey, all at his expense with some gratitude money thrown in, to accept with pleasure and soon hands were shaken, and it was all arranged. The plan was that Jacob, himself, would approach Anna about releasing the holy man's rubble to the Dutchmen. They would depart in a few week's time.

Jacob spent the rest of the day humming and smiling to himself. Come evening, when the rain stopped, he locked up the shop and made his way home to the small apartment in his son's house where he lived, rather uneasily, with the woman, Jeanne, who had nursed him back to health. Walking along the cobbled street, or stumping along would be more accurate, he reminded himself that he was an old man with one leg and how was he planning to go up the mountain to the hermitage to see Anna where he supposed she would have gone for the summer. Had Lootjens said something about a helicopter? He'd said a lot, he'd brimmed with words, beginning with his kind words about the book which began to assume the shape in Jacob's mind of outright flattery. Yes, flattery to soften him up for this trip, the evil intent of which, Jacob now fully realized, was for Jacob to aid him in ripping off the hermitage rubble for Lootjens to profit from. And Jacob, like a fool, like a child, had been taken in, caught up, swept away. The idea of seeing Anna and the children again had blinded him to the ramifications.

Now the color in his cheeks was from shame, not pleasure. He'd fallen prey to the machinations of a man he hadn't liked in the first place, the very man who had stolen from Anna before. He had gotten old and soft and simple-minded. How Joe would laugh at his becoming a patsy for praise.

Not only had he believed the man in his plaudits for the book but he'd begun to think that it would change the world, as if it wasn't Joe who was doing the world-changing but old Jacob-know-nothing with his book about Joe. Jacob shook his head but, thinking of Joe laughing with him about Lootjens, made him laugh, too. Well, he'd made the deal with the man and he'd stick to it. The great thing was that he'd see Anna and the children, let the rubble fall where it may. He would be honest and mention the purpose of his trip to Anna. She would say no, and that would, he hoped, be that. In any case nothing could hurt Anna when the holy bodyguard was once again at her side.

Chapter 25
T'ai Chi

Alim, whose photo shop was now the tea shop, had a remarkable son named Drang. He had been the champion martial artist of the country, and then gone on to fight in the nine years war with their neighbor, becoming a General by the end of it. Now the people were agitating for him to lead the country as Prime Minister. But first, his father and mother were agitating for him to come home, stay a while with them, and choose a bride from his home town.

Drang liked to visit Anna in her kitchen where she talked with him in the same easy-going way she talked to everyone.

"I like being in this room where I spent so much of my own childhood," Drang said. "I see Melissa and Jimmy running in and out or sitting here drawing pictures and remember my young self."

For such a worldbeater, Drang was a normal sized guy with normal sized muscles and an unassuming presence but when he moved one noticed something different about him, something uncanny, and when you looked into his eyes you saw something different, too.

Now he was relaxed in a straight-back chair that he had tilted against the wall.

"Joe always said …"

"Anna, you can't tell me anything Joe said that I don't know. All the kids of this town lived and breathed Joe's wisdom and don't forget my father lived two years with him in the hermitage and what eight year old boy was there, too, whenever he could get away from school?"

Anna smiled.

"Joe taught me T'ai Chi and it was my incorporating those secrets into our own martial art that made me a champ. 'A force of four ounces deflects a thousand pounds.'"

"Oh?" Anna turned from the sink, wiped her hands dry and hung up the cloth. "How is that?"

"Imagine a rhinoceros stampeding down the river path when a feather flutters by, distracting him, throwing him off balance. Despite all appearances to the contrary, winning is not to the swiftest or the strongest. It is knowing your opponent and how to respond to your opponent, when to bend or straighten, move or be still, yield or adhere. It is knowing when to appear and when to disappear. It is breath, spirit, agile mind, and internal force. All this is instruction for hand-to-hand combat or army-to-army and I was taught it by Joe. Now if he had only taught me how to run a country..."

Drang smiled and his dark face flooded with light. The difference between his smile and Anna's was that Anna's face was always alight.

"I'm jealous. Joe didn't teach me T'ai Chi."

"With you, his time was short. He had more valuable lessons."

"Yes, he did." Now Anna's face turned a tiny bit dark, the merest shadow of a darkness as she thought how she was failing Joe. What was she doing with his teachings? Baking buns.

As if reading her mind, which she had noticed he was prone to do, Drang said, "My father tells me that you have given up all thoughts of being the holy man's replacement and are going to keep running the tea shop."

"Yes."

"This is good. It's only when you completely realize you are not ready for something that you begin to be ready."

Another day, Drang came at the end of the afternoon and said, "Let's go for a pony ride on the mountain."

"What a nice idea. Let me just arrange for the kids."

"They're all set. They've gone to Ezla's to make pots."

"Are the ponies going to tolerate our sitting on them for very long," Anna asked when they got to the pasture.

"Oh yes, I know just the ones to choose."

"Were they here nine years ago when you last came?"

"Our ponies live twenty five years."

An hour later, Anna was seated bareback on a buff colored pony with white markings, Drang on a dappled chestnut, riding on a path that was new to her where the ponies tripped happily along, keeping their pirouettes, leaps, and fancy footwork to a minimum. Instead of going up the mountain they were traversing it -- splashing through creeks, and winding along spidery trails. They came to what Anna could only describe to herself as a bower.

A vine similar to a wisteria only with rose colored blossoms instead of white or blue, had climbed from tree to tree forming a tunnel that widened to a room-like space. Looking up she could see only small patches of blue sky between the predominant pink and green. Drang slipped to the ground and lifted Anna from her pony enclosing her in his arms. She put her arms around his neck and they stood heart to heart, naturally. Soon the rosy glow illuminated Drang's battle-scarred skin and Anna's snowy skin that was spattered with tiny freckles. Soon, her red hair entwined with his black locks as the green tendrils around and above them sought out each other, and their limbs cleaved to one another just as the tough, thick vines had found the slender tree branches.

Hours passed. When they talked, their conversation murmured like the pollen-gathering bees. When they were silent, nature hushed with them, and if they released unearthly cries, surrounding fauna, including the ponies, were approving and undisturbed. They even slept quick, sweet sleeps together as if wanting to experience, in their few stolen hours, everything that matrimony would have awarded. They never stopped being in each other's arms. When the rosy glow dimmed, turned violet, amber, then gray, they dressed, mounted their patient ponies, and set out for home. The ponies knew the way in the darkness as animals always do, and these ponies knew how to choose pathways that would allow the lovers to travel side by side. It was darkest night when Drang returned Anna to her tea shop. Standing at her door, they repeated words already spoken, "If I had chosen a young bride as my father wished, she would have followed me anywhere. But you and I have separate paths to take, equally important ones. We can not possibly take them together - not I with you, nor you with me. And so, Anna, this must be goodbye."

"Yes," Anna said.

"I hope I will be able to come back over the years and see you again, and again."

"Even if it's goodbye forever, I am full of joy."

"Maybe a child will come of this. What then?"

"More joy, Drang."

"When we are old and have fulfilled our destinies, we will build a house high on the mountain, and be together at last."

"How old? Do you think forty will be old enough?"

Drang laughed.

A final embrace, blessed by a sliver of crescent moon.

The next morning, scooping oatmeal, Jimmy asked Anna, "Where did you and Drang go?"

"We rode the ponies on the mountain to a new place. I wonder if I could find it again. It was so pretty."

"What did you do?" Melissa asked.

"He taught me T'ai Chi."

Jimmy and Melissa asked what that was. "Two people play together, one trying to unbalance the other. It is learning when to bend, when to stand straight, when to be still and when to move, when to hold on with all your might and when to surrender."

"I can do all that," Jimmy said.

"Yes you can. And you learn to use your breath, spirit, mind, and internal strength rather than brute force. When you get good at it, you can appear and disappear."

"Wow. I bet Drang's really good at it. Hey, where did Melissa go?"

"I've disappeared," she said from under the table.

"Me, too," Jimmy said, slipping down from his chair.

Drang, too, thought Anna, but I'm not sad. I'm full of internal strength. One never really loses any loved one through death or other disappearance. They're all engraved on our hearts, making us strong.

Chapter 26
Whores

"Now, Anna, I don't know if you're the holy woman or not and I don't care. All I know is that here in this town everyone says you're really nice, have common sense, and give good advice. I'm from the big city where I'm married with four children and a husband who goes with whores."

The woman was in her forties, Anna would say, neatly dressed in clothes that were good but subdued, as were her jewels. She had an open intelligent face. She had found Anna as Anna was returning to the tea shop from the farmer's market. Now they sat together on a bench near a splashing fountain. Little birds pecked at crumbs by their feet and an old dog bathed in the sun with his feet in the air.

"I didn't find out about the whores myself.

Some reporters kindly informed me and the rest of the city in a story they did on prominent men. I was shocked and appalled. Why did he go to the whores? This I never asked him but it might have had to do with shoes. I remember early in our marriage he asked me if I might wear stilletto heels during our lovemaking and I didn't oblige."

Anna listened quietly. The woman's tale was in full flood.

"Naturally he wanted me to stand beside him during his ignominy the way all the fool women do who are wives of politicians -- and say what a fine man he is and how I love him dearly and how this brief aberration of character, due to a mild depression, has only deepened our love and solidified our marriage." She voiced an expletive having to do with elimination from male cows.

Anna listened and excused herself for planning an evening soup with one part of her mind - soup for a hot summer night: perhaps garlic, cucumber, yoghurt ...

"I left the bum. I became an advocate for prostitutes. Do you know that these women, in large percent, were abused as children and they continue to be abused now even though they get paid for it with whatever the pimps choose to dole out to them? Not to mention the fact that most of them are still children. They'll never live to become women my age that's for certain, because most are diseased, in many cases fatally, with no medical care, and continue to work regardless. Thankfully, my husband is unscathed, as am I. I am trying to legalize the profession and my husband, who survived the scandal without me, and still has power, is abetting me in this serious task. He realizes now that for his own amusement he was preying on the weak and desperate. And so, the joke is, I feel now that he is a fine man, a splendid man, that our love has deepened and if I return to him, our marriage will have grown stronger." She laughed. "And, yes, I have decided to return to him. So why, Anna, have I come you in supplication? I think you can tell me what I need to know."

Anna brought her mind away from the summer soup. "You are afraid to demean yourself."

"Uh ..."

"But don't be. Your husband knows now what a strong and noble woman you are. Tell yourself you are willing to be playful for the good of the marriage."

"So ... I should get a pair ..."

"Definitely. Why not purchase an array?"

Chapter 27
Agoraphobia

"Anna, I live here in the village and up until recently lived a sequestered life. I was saddled by fears of something terrible happening to me if I left my home, where my mother and grandfather saw to all my wants, where I was busy and happy reading books, and painting miniatures. We have a walled garden that I was able to venture out into to take a little sun without the sky falling on top of me."

He was a young man, thin, with big eyes, and definitely jumpy, unable to sit still, constantly looking about him for possible assassins or plummeting pieces of sky.

"I heard about you and your tea shop and got it in my head that I would come to see you for help, but even thinking of such a preposterous move practically gave me a heart attack. The adrenalin rushed through me in a mighty torrent. I would pass out in a fit of dizziness before I even got to the door. Still, the thought would present itself, and one day I got to the door. The day came when I got through the door. "What are you doing?" my mother screamed, but my grandfather came and stood beside me on the stoop and said, "Good boy." We stood together on the stoop and watched the world go by. I saw one or two of my classmates from school and we shouted greetings back and forth. A week later I made it down the steps before collapsing. My mother begged me to give up my crazy behavior, reminding me how ill and frail I was, but my grandfather said ..."

"Good boy." Anna finished.

"Yes, and now that I was down the steps and out in the world, so to speak, some of my old friends from when I was little, came and talked to me. I told them my plan. 'Oh, Ganjui," they said, 'don't you know that first you have to go to Ezla's pottery studio and make a tea cup with which you will drink the tea at Anna's tea shop.' Oh, no! I said, how can I do that? 'Easy for you, they told me. You're already an artist.' I told them I didn't even know where Ezla's studio was and when they explained it was the other side of the park, I sighed deeply. It was a long way for me to go and I would have to practice going a little way toward it each day."

Anna nodded. She was interested in this tea cup business. She knew that more and more cups kept appearing on the olive trees, and in this way she was saved from having to do dishes for her shop, but somehow she hadn't realized that everyone was making their own. "Do people have their names on their cups?" she asked.

"Why, no. Everyone gets to use any cup that's available but it wouldn't be fair if they hadn't contributed a cup."

"How marvelous. So then what happened?"

"Well, already I was pretty transformed and beginning to have a social life with old friends and new ones I met on my walks through the park and then at the studio but I still hadn't made it to the tea shop."

"Because?"

"Because everyone said I had to go up the mountain first. It was kind of a rite of passage. It didn't matter how far up. It had to do with the holy man in some way and his being dead now and going there to greet his spirit. They all said it would please Anna."

"It does please me."

"And that took another month because, you see, I still had no muscles. The trip to Ezla's was nothing in comparison to climbing the mountain trail, or lack of trail. I got it in my mind I wouldn't come to see you until I'd gone all the way to the top."

"Congratulations. You look very strong. Of course I don't know how you looked before. But, Ganjui, you have made a real pilgrimage into living a good life."

"Which is what I was going to ask you how to do, but found out by myself on the way to you, Anna. It's like a miracle."

"The human body and mind is a miracle. Ganjui, please sit down at the table and I will bring you some lovely tea for your cup."

"Thank you and, bye the way," he said before he left her kitchen. "I only live next door. If the tea shop wasn't next door, I never would have thought of coming in the first place."

Chapter 28
Credo For Success

Meanwhile, back in Austria, Jacob was making ready for his trip to the mountain to see Anna and, ostensibly, to obtain the holy rubble for Lootjens to sell at auction.

One afternoon his oldest son, Franz, appeared for the first time in the bookstore of his youngest son, Bertil. Jacob was behind the counter, manning the shop.

"Franz, what a pleasure." He came around to embrace his first son who looked extremely woeful. "How are you?"

"Not so good. I am soon to be bankrupt if I do not sell the house and stores to pay off my debts."

"I am sorry to hear that. Will you have some coffee?"

"No, thank you." Franz gazed around the store, perhaps wondering if it were a successful emporium masquerading as a shabby shop. "How is Bertil doing? I wonder if he has some savings he could invest to keep my last store afloat."

Jacob smiled. "Bertil makes just enough money to support himself, his wife, his old father, and most of his friends."

"Well, he must make a lot of money then."

"No, Franz. He doesn't need a lot of money because he has a heart of gold."

Franz frowned. "It is not fair. You come back home to Austria and instead of helping me out of my difficulties, you come and help Bertil run his crummy little shop."

"On the contrary. It is Bertil who has helped me. The poorest of my sons took me in when I was down and out. It is the least I can do in return to keep the shop open when he is away buying books."

Franz, who, thanks to his father, not so long ago, had five gleaming multi-leveled, bustling, department stores and a million dollars for spending money, felt bitter and wronged. "You have always favored Bertil," he whined.

"Franz. Be a man. Pull yourself up by your

bootstraps. Learn from your failure. Any one who is a success in life, has suffered failures because they have the mentality to take on risk. It was my fault that I handed those stores to you instead of letting you build a business for yourself. You weren't ready for such a huge responsibility. Now you must quickly sell off your puffed-up house and pay off your debts, trying to save the one store with which you can build up the business again. That is, if you like merchandising. Otherwise, think what you do want to do, and begin afresh. Making a new start is always exciting."

"This is extremely hard on my wife and children."

"Of course it is. But she was an energetic, capable woman when you married her. Invite her to be your partner. I bet she was feeling pretty bored just buying things. Tell her to start her own little second hand shop, selling off all you've acquired. I guarantee she'll have fun."

"This is a good idea."

Jacob could see in his son a physical response to his pep talk. Franz stood a little taller, his chin a little higher. He even seemed a little less bald on his pate now that his head didn't droop. "And you, Franz, instead of mooning about looking for money ..."

"Of course Karl has money to burn!" he said jealously. "He sits there and warms his hands over it." The little jolt of interest in life that Jacob had inspired and which had appeared as sparks in his lifeless eyes, now subsided dully into dollar signs as before. "I hate him. I have to say I pretty much hate everyone these days. Especially myself for making such a mess."

"Franz, go back out into the arena. You were a good business man when you worked for me. You have the right stuff. You can turn things around. Just like when you're a kid. You fall down. You pick yourself up. And, remember the main thing."

"What is that?"

"To treat everyone you deal with as a holy person."

"Is this the new credo for success?"

"Absolutely."

"I haven't come across it on the financial pages."

"It will soon be there. And never forget that you, Franz, are a holy person, too."

"That's a laugh."

"Wait and see."

"Perhaps I will have that cup of coffee after all."

"Good and here comes Bertil. I can see the smoke from the exhaust of his very old truck. He will be so pleased that you have come to visit him and that you are not looking for money."

"Right." Franz smiled. "Because holy men such as myself don't do that."

Jacob handed him his coffee and poured a slug of brandy in it to celebrate. In his mind he apologized to Joe for using the pull yourself up by your bootstraps homily as Joe didn't believe in harsh admonitions as an improvement to character. Although, Jacob remembered, there was a time Joe pulled a lazy monk up off his bed by his robe and gave him a good shaking. Joe was able to do that sort of thing in a playful way that left the monk dazed but putty in his hands.

Chapter 29
D-d-d-death

Jacob decided to go see Karl, his miser son, before he left for the mountain, to see how he was progressing, or not progressing.

Karl was alone in the same stark apartment whose focal point was the computer with lines of minuscule numbers displayed, to inform him of his financial status.

Jacob set his jacket over the monitor so that Karl could give his father his attention. "I am sorry to find you so, Karl. I had hoped your wife and children were back with you, that there would be some life here."

"She wouldn't have me."

"Why was that?"

"Because of my ... obsession she called it. She

couldn't understand it as my business, that I put in my hours just as any man does."

"I see." Jacob watched his son pace around the small room, his eyes darting glances at the covered monitor. He glowered at his father. He didn't ask Jacob to sit down, but Jacob did, nor did he offer him anything. "Karl, you strike me as a man who is full of anxiety."

Karl said nothing for several minutes that stretched liked hours. Finally, he threw up his hands and tugged at his hair. "I ... I am very scared. That's the truth."

"Are you scared to lose your money?"

"No." Now he plopped down in the worn armchair next to Jacob and laughed harshly. "To tell the truth, I could handle my wealth with both hands tied behind my back and a blindfold on, spending all of forty five minutes a day. But somehow, when I bury my mind in the figures, I am at ease. I am not afraid. I guess it is like a drug, an escape from the horror of ..." He grimaced, "what is to come."

"It is a sad case that those who fear death the most end by having no life."

"Please don't even say the D word."

"I have been thinking about you and realizing

that it must go back to that skiing accident you had when you almost lost your life. It is always a terrible shock when we first have the realization we are mortal."

Karl put his head in his hands, covering his eyes. "It is the abyss, the nothingness that's so horrifying. And I refuse to pretend to believe in God and an afterlife. I gave up fairy tales long ago."

"I understand. And yet, finally, it is knowing that our death will come, and can come at anytime, that gives life its sweetness and makes each day sublime. But only if you have a life of affirmation, not negation, only if you are loving yourself and others."

"It is easy for you. Everything has always been easy for you."

"Not so. I have been full of the despair of self-hate to where I wanted to end my life."

"No!"

"Yes. Then I met Joe, the holy man. He gave me heart. Then his monks gave me a task to fulfill that gave life meaning."

"And does life still have meaning now that you are down to no money and one leg, now that you are old and ugly?"

"It seems to." Jacob smiled. "Karl, if you could

have a spiritual community of sorts of which you are a part, even if only the people on your street, your neighborhood merchants, the bar you go to, the soccer club you belong to. In other words friends to raise your spirits, to care about - it need not be a religiously oriented community although a place to worship can be nice even if you don't believe. There is actually a solace that comes from pretending to believe that sometimes even ends in belief. My son, you have isolated yourself and you are full of dread."

"But d-d-death – there, I have said the word." Perspiration broke out on his brow.

"Good. That is a beginning. Keep saying the word until you are weary of it. Let the it hold no more horrors for you than would the word bread. Bread gives us life. So does death which teaches us impermanence and therefore what is meaningful, money being the least of it."

"Please don't malign my money. It is all that I have left."

Was Karl making a joke? That would be fantastic.

Jacob powered on.

"I beg of you, don't greet death, with the awful knowledge that you haven't lived and loved. Begin with your children. Even if your wife will not have you, you are the only father they have."

"They'll soon have another by the look of things."

Karl was a hard nut to crack. "So what? Go to them today and tell them you love them. Just as I have come to you today to tell you I love you. Be there for them when they first realize life ends, and teach them courage."

"Give me a task, then."

"Good. I am going away. Help your brother Bertil in his store now and then. Help your brother Franz get his life on a new footing. I am not asking you to give them any money."

"No fear of that," Karl said and Jacob thought he could detect just the tiniest twinkle to his eyes. If he could begin to laugh at himself and his miserliness, he was on his way. And Jacob could go on his way. On his way rejoicing.

Chapter 30
Shame and Remorse

Chen had summoned Errol for a conference at his pool, but hadn't said to bring his bathing suit since only Chen was permitted to use the Olympic-sized, indoor waterway. As Errol approached, taking in the fabulous architectural details, he wondered again why Chen wanted adobe rubble embedded with his ultra-modern materials.

Chen was powering up and down the pool like a seal, doing flip turns at each end. Errol watched enviously. He didn't announce himself. Chen would know he was here. He knew everything. Plus, who would dare to be late to a meeting with him? Errol pondered this. It was certainly not fear of punishment for he was a benign ruler. Fear of disfavor, he guessed. One ardently wanted to be in Chen's good graces. Perhaps the word ruler was the key. He was not a holy man, he was a holy sovereign. They all strove to be like him and be liked by him, longed to have his beauty, intelligence, and mystical powers which he assured them they could have if they followed his path.

Errol stood by the pool's edge and eventually Chen levitated out of the water and stood beside him, his lithe, muscular body glistening, his face happy and relaxed from the exercise.

"Errol I am having second thoughts about sending you on this mission for Joe's rubble."

"Why?"

"I see that since I told you about Anna's situation, you are full of shame and remorse." He raised a hand to hush Errol's response. "Shame-and-remorse is not a good thing. It bows down my emissary. One does not do good work burdened with shame and remorse."

"But I want to go. I want to see Anna and the children. You said it would be good for me to go begging. You said that she is well despite my behavior. Seeing her will relieve my ..er...shame and remorse." Eric smiled because the two words, through repetition had become funny sounding .

"There is another reason. I have discovered

that there is a Dutchman who is also after Joe's rubble - his purpose being highly nefarious. This man is a true villain. He is the man who, with a band of thugs, went up to the hermitage last summer and pillaged it. They took everything that wasn't nailed down. Anna was alone with the children and helpless."

"Oh my God!" Errol clasped his brow. "You didn't tell me that part of the story. This gets worse and worse. What a nightmare. Were they hurt?"

"No, Anna with her kindness and dignity knew just how to handle them."

Shame and remorse were no longer funny-sounding to Errol. He was consumed by both, overcome by weakness. He looked around for somewhere to sit but they remained at the edge of the pool.

"It is I who am the consummate villain," Errol said with quavering voice. He tried to pull himself together. "But all the more reason I must go. I'll throw myself at Anna's feet and beg forgiveness."

"That's a great plan. Beg her forgiveness and then ask her for the rubble? I don't think so. Even if there were no rubble involved in your course of action, why throw the burden of your shame and remorse on Anna. Handle it yourself."

"I wish I could at least bring her money."

"Don't be an idiot. She has no use for money, especially blood money."

"Blood money you call it? Good grief. My life is turning to horror. Is that why I haven't been paid, because the money has blood all over it?"

"Yes."

"Because I've been living the good life at Anna's expense."

"Yes."

"You bribed me away from my responsibilities and I accepted the bribe."

"Yes."

"Anna thought it was great for me and my career. She said, "Go."

"Being Anna, yes."

"I will throw myself at her feet."

"Don't imagine you are so important to her. Her happiness does not depend on you."

"What shall I do?"

Chen smiled. "You can go to her. But I will go with you. Together we will see how things turn out. Meanwhile, make yourself strong. In your stance, let your feet connect to the earth. Let the soles of your feet grow long roots so that you cannot be toppled." So saying, Chen touched Errol's shoulder with his little finger and Errol, unbalanced, flapped his hands in the air helplessly, then fell into the pool. Chen walked away without looking back.

Well, thought Errol, something good has come of this torture session. I got to go swimming in the emperor's pool.

Chapter 31
Sensitivity

Jacob had not yet told his house-mate, Jeanne, about his expedition, now imminent, to the mountain because, as soon as he had ceased to be an invalid, she had subjected him to emotional scenes when he wanted to go anywhere without her - to see his sons in Vienna, or even to go down the street to the Gasthaus for a beer. He would try various maneuvers to appease her which shamed him and often dug him deeper into the emotional hole.

Jacob feared no man or beast, no dire situation, neither sickness, nor death, but still foundered before the tearful eye, tremulous lip, the quavery voice. Even knowing they were but weapons in the arsenal of domestic tyranny, he was helpless under their attack. Even knowing that sensitivity was often no more than a fine honing of greediness and controlling-ness, he knew not how to engage, let alone win, against it, for the sensitive soul is deceiving him or her self. She has grown to believe in these tears and quavers as true signs of psychic wounds – and why should she not believe in them since they are so effective in spouse control?

He remembered Anna's hearty response to Errol's invitation to Universe-city: 'But of course! You must go at once!' And, if tears came later regarding Errol's abandonment, they were for her own solace only, not to grapple her husband to her with hoops of watery steel.

"Have I mentioned to you, Jeanne, that I am off for a while on a commission for Lootjens?" He had to cleave to the commission angle as to go simply for love of Anna, Jimmy, and Melissa, would be domestic suicide.

Jacob, fortifying himself for the coming scene, also preached kindness to his heart. Bear in mind, he told himself, how warm and loving she has been to this old soldier, how she nursed him back to manhood from his lost leg, and soothed his excruciating phantom pain.

But have I not repaid that in full. It is time to move on. Past time. I must be brave.

"I did hear of this trip from Bertil," Jeanne said, "but scoffed at the notion, saying my darling can't go anywhere with one leg."

"I'm getting along pretty well now on my crutches."

Out came the handkerchief from her pocket as quick as a knife from its sheathe. Paying no heed to his last remark, she continued. "Also, I told Bertil Jacob would never leave me when I have come to depend on him so utterly." She fixed him with stricken eyes.

He fixed her back with a glare, saying gruffly, "Jacob would and he will. I am going tomorrow."

Jeanne fell back with hand to heart, handkerchief to eyes, "Oh!"

"Yes. I have my ticket and need only to throw a few things in a bag."

"But how long ...?" came the stifled cry.

"As long as it takes," said Jacob, vowing to maintain his vital gruffness and not cave in. "As long as it takes."

Shoulders back, head high, he stumped away from her flood of tears that soon turned to a scream, "You don't love me. You never loved me," which he understood to be a cry from her heart that really meant: "Foiled! Foiled!"

He thought he was home safe, or away safe, but she followed him to the bedroom where he was packing his small bag. She fell to her knees, then to the floor, putting her hands around his ankle, covering his shoe with her tears.

Seeing her seem to utterly abase herself in this way might have touched his hardened heart except that he realized it would only take one tug on his ankle to bring him violently down on the base of his fragile spine. Then he would be bedridden as before.

One crutch was on the bed, the other under his arm on the side that had no leg but he had no way to brace himself if she pulled his leg from under. If he appeased her, even with false promises, he might be safe but he refused to shame himself. With either hand he could strike her into immobility but he had vowed never again to hurt someone for any reason.

As he remained unresponsive to her posture and tears, he felt her hands tighten on his ankle. The sweat stood out on his brow. He bent his knee and thrust his body backward to the bed, landing there on his back in a sprawl, but unharmed. His foot brushed her face as it flew upward, but made no mark.

She reported him to the police for kicking her in the face but, "How?" asked Jacob, "does a one-legged man kick someone? You see," he said to the officer, "she was taking my leaving her to go on a business trip as a personal blow."

"Yes," the policeman agreed. "We men must appear heartless at times. But women are so sensitive, you know."

"I know," Jacob said, sighing deeply. "Do I ever!"

Jacob tried to think how he could have handled things better. One tries to live right and do right, he thought, but it all gets tricky and messy when dealing with a love relationship, or what is, in effect, a loveless relationship.

Chapter 32
Facing One's Face

"Lootjens, I have decided to go alone as your secret ambassador to collect the rubble."

"Absolutely not."

"You are known and hated in the village. It is to your advantage to stay here."

"I shall go incognito. A simple disguise."

"Impossible. Not with your teeth."

"What about my teeth?

"Look in the mirror, man."

For once he and Jacob had not met in the bookstore but were at a sidewalk café having Viennese coffee and pastry.

"I never look in mirrors," Lootjens said. "I shave with an electric razor, sitting in an armchair, feeling my face as I remove the night's stubble."

"Really? So do I." They gazed at each other, surprised and perhaps uneasy, at finding this similarity between them.

"I've never liked my looks," Jacob admitted.

"I have. When I was young I was tall and handsome. The Dutch have the tallest men per capita of any country, you know. I think you are a tall man, too, although you are always sitting down."

Jacob smiled. "I don't want to tower over you and make you uncomfortable."

Lootjens gave his fake laugh to acknowledge what he perceived as a joke.

Jacob said, "Have you ever come upon a mirror image of yourself by accident, in a store window perhaps, and not recognized yourself. This is common with everyone."

"Yes, yes. I believe so. How interesting. But I eased my distress by telling myself it was another person. Explain this phenomenon."

"I think people prepare an image in their mind's eye when they approach their mirror, of the face they used to have and want still to have. They are ready with their pretend-face by the time the mirror claims it. When they come on their image by chance, they have not prepared the mirror with the right reflection and so for a second it is unrecognizable."

Later, remembering this exchange, Lootjens went to a store, bought a large hand mirror and took it home to look into, particularly in respect to his teeth.

Once there, he whisked it from the bag and snagged his reflection with no preparation.

Good God, the teeth! How big! How snaggled and stained! This must be what was meant by getting long in the tooth. Wide in them, too. His lips ceased to meet except when purposely pulled down from above. The lips themselves had lost the fulness and shapeliness of his youth, were drawn thinly back as if in a snarl. His hawk's nose had blossomed and fruited into a potato, a red potato. The lustrous eyes were, yes, face it, piggy - impouched between forehead and cheeks.

If he had known of this facial misfortune he would not have carried himself like the tall, bold, attractive man he believed himself to be and instead would have sidled cringing into rooms, trying to make his self small, his hand held protectively over his tooth-filled mouth. But no, he must not make himself small if all he had left was his height.

Yes, Lootjens decided sadly, Jacob must go without him for the rubble? Nothing could disguise this misfortune of a face.

He looked again in the mirror? Who was this man looking back at him. Who was the man looking at the reflection? Where was the Lootjens of yore with the world at his feet?

What if the young Lootjens was only a figment of his imagination? Image? Imagination? It was the same. After all, perhaps at any age, one only imagined one's face.

He remembered the saying that a man is responsible for his face after thirty – supposedly because his visage is affected by his character. He was well over forty; too late to alter his outward alteration but he still could change himself from within.

In the end, people don't respond to a person's looks but to something else. Jacob was extremely likeable. Lootjens knew that he, even at his most affable, was not, nor had he cared. This whole holy man business was weird. He didn't get it. He didn't want to get it. But, he had to admit he was beginning to like old Jacob. The man had depth. And honesty. He could trust him to go to the mountain without him. And he'd never, never, trusted anyone. If he were to subscribe to the holy man credo he would trust all and sundry. That would certainly be a tricky way to do business. But, he had to admit, it was nice trusting a person, nice liking that person and possibly being liked in return. It was nice that they both did not look in mirrors and shaved the same way.

Chapter 33
Transitions

Anna took what used to be called the Back Trail up the mountain to avoid what seemed to be a lot of people on what used to be the Hermitage Trail. It had been a while since she'd been to Joe's grave vicinity and she wanted to be with him. She took a little detour to "the bower" where she had celebrated life and love with Drang. The blooms were gone from the vine accept for a few faded reminders. She sat a while holding the letters she had received from Drang who was in the capital city five hundred miles away. His words were brief but sweet. She didn't need to read them over, only to feel them in her hands.

Then she proceeded up the mountain, first going again to the sacred ruin which still shone with its miraculous light, still hummed and twittered, crackled and rustled from its natural life within. From there, she wandered down to where she had determined Joe's grave site to be because the lupin, a spring flower, seemed to be forever in bloom there, the boulder birds to be constantly singing.

She shed a few tears in spite of herself, missing so much his actual presence, the wondrous warmth and peace of his personality when he was on earth. She would never stop missing him.

"Well, Joe, you see before you a failed holy woman but a really good tea shop operator. In fact, the mountain and town has recently begun swarming with visitors who have come to set foot on the holy man's mountain and then to refresh themselves with a cup of tea and a bun or two. I am embarrassed at how much money I'm making. I think I will send Melissa and Jimmy home to Ireland to visit with their grandparents before school starts. And of course I will contribute to the needs of the town's poor. I shall stay here, Joe. Here is my home. I know that now for sure. I am happy. The children are happy. I like them growing up in an non-materialistic society such as this is. Don't be disappointed that I can not be what you hoped for me. The main thing is that I myself am not disappointed. I realize I am just an ordinary person. I will always try to be as good as I can and as helpful to others as I can. I will always feel proud and even a little bit exalted that you chose me to be by your side at the last and then to replace you. What you have instead is the whole holy mountain to replace you. You believed that it was the pilgrim's stay on the mountain, as they wended their way to you, that healed them from their ills and sorrows, and so it does still. It seems everyone enters my tea shop with a smile on their face. The funny thing is that there is a line to the shop. Not a line of thousands such as yours was in previous summers, perhaps thirty or forty people, coming down the mountain instead of going up, but they must be doing each other good."

Anna talked on, about the shop, the townspeople, the prisoners, the children in the park, her own children, the proliferation of kerchiefs the three crippled women continued to produce, and as she talked she began to see the entire year that had passed, from her abandonment at the hermitage, the looting of it, the transfer to town and the evolving of her shop and was amazed at the fulness of life, amazed at the twists and turns it takes just in the space of a year. She thought awhile about the transitions in life, both physical and emotional. Life never stops moving, from moment to moment, day to month to year, and there is always change within and without. If only people who believe they are tired of life, or unable to bear its pain, would allow their hearts to wait and see what happens next.

She told Joe about Drang and the bower, not excusing her behavior but letting it underline her premise that she was an ordinary woman. Such a passionate performance, so spontaneous in its occurrence, certainly would be considered atrocious in a holy person.

After this disclosure she waited to see if the lupin wilted away and the birds stopped singing but there was no such sign. Instead there was a small shower with something of the same sparkling rain drops that occurred at Joe's funeral so that Anna felt blessed by the gentle dousing. Then, fearful that the sprinkle might presage a similar devastating storm as followed Joe's interment, Anna set off back down the mountain to her home.

On the way back she passed a curious-looking creature, tall, ungainly, dressed in long skirts with a turban swaddling her head. She carried large cloth bags in either hand that appeared to be empty.

What could she be gathering in such containers? It wasn't the mushroom season. When Anna said good afternoon and paused as if to chat, the woman pressed her lips tightly together and soldiered on. Back at the tea shop Anna was greeted by marvelous news, "Jacob is here!" said Jimmy. "And he only has one leg!" said Melissa, scooping Jimmy's news, her eyes full of wonder.

And there stood dearest Jacob in the kitchen doorway, emanating his amazing strength and kindness, his huge love. She walked right into his open arms and they wet each other with their tears, another gentle dousing.

Chapter 34
In The Line

"I am Anna's husband."

"Sure you are. And I'm the king of Siam."

Chen watched on, amused, as Errol tried to wangle his way to the head of the line.

"I'm the Line Master," the woman, who wasn't really the king of Siam, said. "I organize the line and take care of trouble-makers, just as I did for the holy man's line his last summer. These are the rules. No butting in. No saving places. No making trouble. No pulling rank by claiming false connections to the holy woman."

"Tell her, Chen."

The woman, who was full of a benign energy, turned to Chen. "Well?"

"I have known this man, Errol, for a year. He is

not Anna's husband. Not even remotely. Come on, Errol, let's go to the end of the line. Maybe we'll learn something."

"That man, Chen," said a woman in the line to the man in front of her, both of whom had been listening to the dispute," could be the Chen of Universe-city. Don't you think?" She spoke in French, as did he in his response.

"I couldn't say. All Asians look alike."

"Oh boy, I can see why you've come to consult the holy woman. Narrow-mindedness."

"Come on, Letitia. We've been talking together for a couple of days now. Have I showed any prejudice toward you."

"You mean because you haven't commented on my being fat, or gay, or black?"

"Right. I didn't even notice."

"Which one?"

"Your ... uh ... being black."

They both laughed. And the Line Master, who was listening to them as they had done with her, said in English, "You have to realize that you probably won't get to consult Anna. You may not even see her, although some have and some have even been touched by her. The most you can hope for is to drink a cup of tea made from her own hands, but that in itself seems to be a forceful experience."

"Forceful?"

"Life-changing. For the good of course. For instance, when our friend Letitia here, has sipped the herbal tea, she will no longer feel so important about being gay black and obese. She will come to mention it less and less, no longer feeling bad about it, or good about it, she will just be. And she will let others be."

"Hey! Who said I was obese?"

"Well, it's faster than to say "enormously fat."

"Woman, you got narrow-minded problems of your own. And full-of-your-own-importance problems, too. You better get a dose of that herb tea of Anna's fast."

The line master laughed. "True. But I used to be much worse, believe me." With a little wave, she drifted away.

"Do you think I'm obese?" she asked her line partner, not in an argumentative way, slightly plaintive.

"I suppose there is some way of measuring when someone has crossed over from fat to obese, but I think you should take her advice, just be yourself with no designation. It is your spirit not your body which has gotten you all the way from your country of origin to this strange, straggling line to see a woman who may or may not be able to help you. I keep trying to see a person's spirit, not how they have encased or incarnated it. Or self-labeled it."

"So Asians really all do look alike to you and you really didn't notice I was black. We all just spirits."

"Yes."

"So, when people ask you who you are or what you do, you say ..."

"I am a fellow being."

"But it seems to me that's a label too. The worst kind. A teaching label that's telling everyone how humble you are. Now you have to see Anna about your false humility."

"Can't I just be humble? Does all humility have to be false?"

"Well, what in heck are you going to see Anna about, Mr. Perfect? I am really curious to know."

"I came to see Anna to understand about humility. Because It is my understanding that she doesn't even know she's a holy woman, doesn't even know we are all out here to come and see her."

There was silence between them while the line moved slowly on toward the tea-shop. "And you?" he asked.

"Well, the opposite I guess. You see, I spent all these years feeling bad about myself and now I've taught myself to be proud of myself but I'm hanging on to that pride with all my might, maybe not really believing in it - like you saw the way I caved in at the word obese. I want to see a woman who, okay, maybe isn't a holy woman, but is proud of herself as a woman even though she just spends her days being a mother and serving tea. It's worth coming all this way to see a woman like that. Worth it to me anyhow."

"And it's worth it to me to come all this way to see you. You've opened my eyes to seeing people again, in all their colors and diversity. I have to say life was looking a bit gray, a bit bleak, with us all just being fellow beings."

"Right and also," she laughed, "come to think of it, saying you're a fellow being is just another way of saying you're a loser."

"I am a loser. But you've got to admit, I'm a really humble loser."

"Yes, you are. That's the trouble with words like humility and pride, they both have a bad odor. By pride I'm really meaning dignity and your humility could be ..."

"Handsomeness?" They laughed again.

Chapter 35
The Great Chen

Errol still grumbled. "I refuse to go to the end of the line."

"It will not be necessary," said Chen. "Just follow me."

"There is a way you can get to the tea shop quicker." A man put out his hand to halt Errol, having overheard his desire to do so. "The people go into the shop as soon as there is a tea cup available. The customer washes it and hangs it on one of the olive trees, then the next person can use it. But maybe you can figure a way to bring your own cup. If, as you say you are her husband, you must be from around here, and familiar with the shops."

"How intriguing," Chen said.

"Intriguing, Chen? It's ridiculous. Imagine people waiting for a newly washed tea cup to get into Universe-city."

"It is an adorable scheme," Chen said, thinking of his guards at the city gate.

"Chen! Are you Chen?" said the man, almost sinking to his knees, for Chen was almost as widely known and revered (by people who cared about holiness) as the Dalai Lama.

"It is Chen," said another. "I recognize him."

"Anna should learn of this," said a woman, "that Chen himself is here."

"Anna should learn that her husband is here, too," Errol muttered.

Chen just kept walking toward the end of the line but, as the news spread like wildfire, the line broke up, back-peddled, and followed him instead of going forward. Mob mentality ensued, although it was a small mob, and others followed the followers, not even knowing what they followed, but inspired to do so by a sense of excitement that almost approached panic, so that people who had been calm as lambs in the line began pushing and elbowing with a susurrous sound that could almost be cursing.

Chen came to a knoll, a raised spot on the

ground with a lovely pine tree in the center. He stopped here and leaned against its trunk. Everyone clustered around and sank down on the ground, hoping to be addressed by him in this special time and place, rather than in the vast stadiums where he usually appeared, his visage blown up on a mammoth screen behind him.

But the jarring excitement persisted, and instead of waiting for his words, people shouted questions. Those who were anxious to hear him tried to hush the questioners so that anger arose. "How can you be here?" one called, "I have a friend in your Universe-city who swears you are there."

Now to make things worse, those in the crowd answered the questioners which agitated the silencers, as well as the questioners themselves.

"Chen can be in two places at one time," they shouted. "Everyone knows that." People began to get back on their feet to take a position on this incredible statement. Stories were told of Chen doing impossible acts: disappearing, levitating, even flying. These stories had been witnessed and verified although they were explained away by doubters as mass hypnotism and the eagerness of the zealot to believe all of the one to whom he has committed his devotion. Chen, of all the earth's holy men, was the number one player since the bottom line of his belief system was that the spirit was not confined to the body, but could teach the body to come along with it in all its endeavors, even to living forever.

So far there was nothing to prove him wrong since, no-one-knew how many decades later, Chen, looking thirty, was still not dead

"Teleportation?" one called. "Is that how you do it?"

"No," answered another. "That only transports him from one place to another with the speed of thought which of course Chen can do, but it doesn't leave one of him behind."

Many of Anna's pilgrims had a position to take on this remarkable statement also and it was getting very noisy indeed there on the base of the holy mountain as others rose to their feet and began crying out questions and answers all against the background drone of hushing sounds.

"Chen! Why have you come here?"

"To see Anna," the answerers answered. "He was Joe's teacher and Joe was her teacher. Everyone knows that."

"Let Chen speak," pleaded some. "Stop asking questions. We are missing a great opportunity."

People were not only back on their feet, they were jumping up and down, blocking the view of Chen from the others, and Chen was forgotten in the commotion that now increased to a tumult. He and Errol, laughing, went down the back side of the knoll and down the path to the teashop where two brightly burnished cups hung from the olive tree branch, awaiting their grasp. They followed Letitia and her friend into the shop since those two, being serious students of pride and humility, had been more pleased to go forward to see Anna, than backward to see Chen.

Chapter 36
In the Tea Shop

When Errol stepped into the café, his eyes immediately lit on Anna, who was transformed from the dowdy, little, grieving woman in a wheat-colored robe, who he had left on the mountain more than a year ago. She was resplendent in green silk with threaded-gold trim -- a tunic the women of the town wore on festive occasions. Her red hair, which seemed also trimmed in threads of gold, was out of its kerchief and flowed in waves to her shoulders and down her back. Her previously wan cheeks were flushed pink with happiness, her eyes sparkled, and her teeth gleamed between ruby lips.

She was moving from one person to another where they sat at the long table that Errol recognized from the hermitage, Anna saying a few words to each one, lightly touching their shoulders as if she were a hostess saying, Do you have everything you need? Is everything all right? The late afternoon sun shone through the clean windows, naturally lighting the room. The tea shop was colorful with amateur art work on walls and on shelves around the room. There was a scent of spices combining with the fresh mountain air and the murmur of happy voices was like creek water rippling over stones. It was the voices that distinguished the room from Joe's hermitage where meals, or tea, had always been taken in silence.

The description of Anna that Errol's eyes delivered, especially the ruby lips part was, as if from a romance novel, but it was all true. He was wowed. He remembered Chen saying, don't throw your shame and remorse on Anna, you are not that important to her, her happiness does not depend on you.

Clearly this was true. As was Chen saying: he is not remotely her husband.

His shame and remorse were still wedged within him. He had behaved badly and he wanted her to know that he knew it. He wanted her to care. He wanted to be important to her as he had been for so many years. Maybe, he had forfeited that by forsaking her, and by the brutal letter he had written to her, but maybe when she saw him again, she would be able to forgive him, especially because she had survived so well and was in a position of strength.

Did he wish she had not survived so well? No, no. He wanted her happiness, even if it didn't hinge the tiniest bit on him. She was the mother of his children. She was the woman he had loved since school days. It had been madness to leave her. It had been Chen's doing. Chen admitted as much. Anna knew the man's power. She would understand.

Errol reminded himself how he had almost left her another time, almost taken the children away when she was on her journey with Joe, and there was no Chen mixed into the abandonment then. It was Ezla, whose cab they had gotten in to take to the airport, who had interfered, taking them instead to his pottery studio to await Anna's return.

All this passed through Errol's mind in the space of seconds and then his children were in his arms. "Daddy, daddy, you've come. Look at how big we are. Did you see our tea shop? Daddy. Daddy." Errol gathered Melissa and Jimmy in his arms while the tears poured from his eyes. "Aren't you happy to see us, Daddy? Mom, look! It's Daddy. He's come back."

"Welcome, Errol. Welcome, Chen."

Errol was glad for the tears on his face, glad she could see them. They would speak for his deep feeling. "And Jacob is here, too," Anna said. "It's a glorious reunion. Was it Chen who brought you back, Errol?"

"It was Chen who took me away!" he exclaimed. "And how deeply I regret his power to have done so. Anna ..."

"But I asked if he brought you back." Anna looked at him calmly, waiting.

"Yes" he admitted, realizing the stony truth. "It was Chen who brought me back." And Errol wondered if the whole rubble nonsense was exactly that - nonsense.

"I am so glad," said Anna, igniting Errol's heart so that he reached out his arms for her, but she continued, "because I want you to take the children home to Ireland to see our parents before they start school." She smiled. "Come and say hello to Jacob. He's in the kitchen." She turned and led the way. Errol released his arms to his sides and followed.

But Chen halted him and Errol turned, red in the face. "Chen, I ..I .."

"Don't feel bad for trying to blame me. I did take you away although it was certainly not by force. You came like a lamb to slaughter. However, what happened to throwing yourself at her feet, covering yourself with slimy old blame? Eh? Or, if not, since I did advise against the feet-throwing, what about being a man instead of a mouse? Anna will always love you, although not as she once did, but don't you want her to respect you? Never mind. I understand that you are confused and conflicted. You were unmanned because she's so suddenly gorgeous. It's wonderful what being a holy person will do for one's appearance. One only has to look at me!"

"Chen, wait." Errol looked at him gravely. "Is she truly a holy woman? You would know. Tell me what you think?"

Chen smiled. "We'll find out."

Chapter 37
Depression

After dinner they all sat on at the hermitage table - Chen, Anna, Jacob, Errol, Melissa and Jimmy. Jimmy had fallen asleep with his head on his father's shoulder. Bear was asleep under the table. Melissa, amazingly, was asleep on Chen's lap — amazing not because he disliked children, it was that he didn't really consider them part of the human race, more primate-like. But Melissa had seemed to attach herself to Chen at the outset, not in the annoying way that cats will come to people who don't like them by leaping onto their laps, but in a gentle respectful way that Anna had not observed in Melissa before. At first Anna put it down to Chen's blessed and (damned) charisma that he exerted over all living creatures but it wasn't that. Chen seemed equally drawn to Melissa, equally respectful and gentle.

Jacob was telling them all the story of how Lootjens had come into his life and how, during their acquaintanceship, Jacob's feelings had evolved from wanting to kill him to almost beginning to like him. When Lootjens released his plan for collecting the hermitage rubble to sell at auction over the internet, and asked Jacob to go back to the mountain and pave his way, Jacob seized the chance to come and see Anna.

Anna was having little bells go off in her mind but couldn't clarify what they were signaling. It had been a long, emotional day and she was tired.

"So, I have come under false pretenses as far as Lootjens is concerned. Of course there is no way I would let him have the rubble for such a greedy purpose that is contrary to all Joe felt about himself and his possessions. This is the man that tried to steal everything of Joe's that remained. Still, I feel like a louse because in the end the man had come to trust me - enough to not come along with me and have faith that I would carry out his wishes."

"This man ended by doing a good thing for me and the children." Anna roused herself to say. "The repercussions were hard to handle at first.

But that long, lonely time on the mountain was something I had to go through and then Alim rebuilt the hermitage interior, here in what used to be his photo shop, and came to the mountaintop to get us. Coming to town was what was right for us all. Here we all bloomed. And the hermitage, left to its own, bloomed also."

She told them all of the hermitage metamorphosis. "It isn't even a ruin exactly. Surely the rocks of the foundation are still there but any adobe will have crumbled away. All you can see are vines, bushes, and flowers tangled together and thrumming with life. The construction seems to sing at you and the light! The light ..." Anna tried to describe it but words failed her. "You will just have to come and see it. Let's all go tomorrow. Oh, but Jacob ..."

"I have a helicopter at the airport," Chen said. We can go all together."

"Why do you have a helicopter?" Jacob asked.

"I confess that I, too, came for the rubble." For the first time since Anna knew him, she observed Chen looking uncomfortable. Color surged to his face and he lowered his eyes. Anna was awed. He struggled to speak. "It .. it was just for myself. For my sanity. No, that is too strong a word. For my health, let's say. I thought that if I could have a bit of Joe around me, I would be healed. I thought if I could live within his own walls I would be as Joe was, full of peace and, more importantly, able to enjoy my possessions once again. You see, everything I touched seemed to turn to dross, to dregs and debris. My feet left gray trails on my carpets. My fingerprints turned silver and gold into tin. My cars no longer glittered and gleamed after I drove them even if I had them shined twice a day. The only thing I didn't seem to mar with my person was the water in my pool but I spent so much time there I was getting waterlogged, not to mention wrinkled as a prune.

"Yes, Anna, Joe wanted me to change myself and my Universe-city and I didn't change either. He came and died near me to help me be well, but I ignored his message. You don't have to remind me of this."

"I wasn't going to, Chen. I'm sure Joe didn't expect you to change overnight. These recent manifestations were only symptoms of your illness he recognized was hurting you a year ago."

"Or these current symptoms were because of your guilt at not changing," said Jacob. "But don't you see, man, you're depressed. How could you change anything, the city or yourself, while being so damned depressed?"

"Me depressed? This is impossible."

"Ah! Don't romanticize yourself away from the truth. Turning gold to tin? Forget it. Everything turns gray when you're depressed. Everything loses its shine. I'm an authority. You think because you're the almighty Chen such human ills can't trouble you. Putting rubble in your walls isn't going to improve matters, I promise you."

"What is?"

"I don't know." Jacob smiled the angelic smile that so easily emerged from his craggy, dangerous-looking face. "Maybe having a little girl fall asleep on your lap. I know that's done wonders for me."

"Maybe going to see the hermitage in all its glory," Anna said.

"It could be that it, too, will look gray and lifeless to me," Chen said -- sadly Anna thought. Anna missed jousting with Chen, missed the sparks that had flown between them, actually missed his maddening arrogance and frightening brilliance.

Chen said, "Moreover, it could be, Anna, that the light you see shining from the ruins is the light in your own eyes."

Errol was disenchanted. How did a holy man

get depressed? How did a hero? Was it really something to do with how one lived ones life or only the circuits in the brain misfiring which the appropriate pills could cure. But maybe the pills didn't cure you, only made you settle for living the wrong life, allowing you to think you see colors when there really weren't any.

Errol believed architecture could make life better. The right design enraptured the spirit. Giving a shape to space as something to live in and to look at that lifts the heart was his aim. It was a profession he loved because it was art and business and human relations all rolled into one. He hadn't gotten waylaid working for Chen. He'd learned an enormous amount. He'd worked with new materials, been inventive and imaginative, but concentrated on making things work. He realized that before going to Chen's Universe-City he'd been the depressed one, full of anger and resentment at the seemingly lost time he'd spent at the hermitage, frustrated at losing control of Anna through her allegiance to the holy man. But no time was lost time. It was all for growing and learning. Just as Anna had said about her desolate time alone. What he had lost was Anna, but he would do everything to be her friend and to be a good father to

Melissa and Jimmy from now on. This he pledged to himself.

When they carried the children to their beds and all said good night, embracing each other, and Errol briefly held Anna in his arms, he was overcome by feelings of desire, love, and loss, so that tears again sprang to his eyes and he had to remember his pledge with all his might. He had to hide his tears from her this time and be a man, not a mouse. He and Chen and Jacob went off into the town to the places they had arranged to stay. A crescent moon hung in the sky and an accumulation of stars pierced the darkness. This was a town that was only lit at night by nature. They still hadn't gone in for street lights. "Look at the stars, Chen," Jacob said. "Surely even depression can't dim their glory."

"You'd be surprised," Chen replied.

And Errol felt grateful that, for himself, the stars were knocking his eyes out, almost too beautiful to bear.

Chapter 38
At the Hermitage

The next morning Errol, Chen, Jacob, Anna, Jimmy and Melissa met at the airport and piled into Chen's helicopter which had arrived some hours after his small private jet the day before.

A half hour later they were nearing the top of the mountain. "Have your pilot land somewhere the whirling blades won't hurt the growth around the hermitage."

"There aren't many other level places."

"I know. And we don't want Jacob to have to go too far."

"Don't worry about me. Slow but sure. There's no pain involved. Even my phantom pain is only a phantom."

The pilot found a place a quarter mile or so

from the hermitage, then joined them all on their trek upwards. It was hard for Jacob with no path on which to place his foot and crutches plus the fact that he was unstable-y dizzy with happiness to back on the mountain where he thought he could never return.

Errol was thinking that it was near this place he had run to tell Anna he was going away with Chen. He had felt so happy and she had responded to his big-heartedness, urging him to go, both feeling perhaps that a time apart would be good for them. And it was. Returning to the spot, coming full circle, he felt that it had been good for them both.

The children scampered ahead, their first time back in a year. "We should have brought Bear," Jimmy said. "He's never been."

"Mom, can we go back for Bear?" Melissa asked.

"We'll bring him next time, sweetheart."

When they came upon the ruins it was as Anna had said: all signs of a manmade structure were covered by vines and flowers, bushes and small trees. However, as to her sacred light, the place was lit by the sun when the meandering clouds uncovered it, just like the rest of the mountain, nothing special.

There was still the thrumming sound of life among the tangle – of lizards, birds, insects, maybe rabbits and ground squirrels. And another sound: a keening, whimpering sound that almost seemed to form the word help!

They looked at each other, mystified, and the children drew close to the grownups. "It's a ghost," said Jimmy.

"Joe would never sound like that," said Melissa. "It sounds hurt. And angry."

The pilot and Chen, for whom the place held no power in their memories, carefully circumnavigated the ruin while Errol stayed with his family, feeling amazed at how thoroughly demolished, how thoroughly disappeared, the hermitage was. Jacob stumped off after Chen.

"Come here!" Chen called. Jacob arrived first and found a creature caught in the hermitage web, caught in a thicket of thorns and vines, a creature that seemed neither man nor woman but both, although the sounds it made were more animal than human. "Lootjens!" cried Jacob.

"Yes, yes it is I. I have been caught here for two days. When I heard the helicopter I thought, saved! But how? How would anyone know I was here? Can you get me out? Did you bring clippers?

If I try to move I get stabbed. Do you have food and water? I am starved and dehydrated."

"Lootjens. You are wearing a dress."

"Yes, yes, it is my disguise, Jacob, and I kept my mouth utterly closed. And here you have come with the helicopter to get the rubble just as you promised. I didn't trust you after all. I couldn't. It is not in my nature to trust. I am not a holy man. I came by myself with bags to collect it in. But there is no rubble. Only these blasted ropes of vines and slashing rose branches and multiple things that sting and burn. Help me."

"Shall we help him, Chen?"

"I think not. We can ask Anna."

"Anna is so forgiving. Too forgiving for such a one as this."

"Jacob, cried Lootjens, " we are friends, not? Did not we nearly become friends?"

"Is this the consummate villain?" Errol appeared at Chen's side.

"In the flesh," said Chen. "The rather flagellated flesh."

Jacob turned his back to Lootjens and said softly to Chen, "After all, he was right not to trust me." Chen replied, "Which does not in the least make it right for him to come and steal as he had done before."

Now Anna and the children came and gazed at the trapped man-in-a-dress. Anna recognized it as the gross, tight-lipped woman who had passed her on the mountain without a greeting and as the Dutch man who had looted the hermitage.

"Stop looking at me as if I were an animal in a zoo. Get me out. Please. I am begging now. I am dying of hunger and thirst. I am bleeding.."

"And his dress is torn, too," said Melissa which made everyone but Lootjens laugh.

"I have a solution," Chen spoke. "We will get him out. We will put him in the helicopter and my pilot will take him ..."

"To the hospital!" Lootjens cried.

" ... to the airport and to a plane that will make his connection back to The Netherlands."

"First making a stop at my hotel for my clothes," Lootjens added hastily to the pilot.

"No," decreed Chen. "He will return home in this dress, hopefully an object of scorn. And Sam," Chen said to his pilot, "Be sure he takes nothing from the helicopter. Search him thoroughly."

"Yes, Sir."

"And then return here to get us."

After asking Anna to take the children away to the other side, Chen and the pilot pulled a howling

Lootjens violently from his snare. Not only did this make him bleed more, in a superficial way, but now his dress was really torn.

"Jacob?" Lootjens looked at him with appeal in his eyes. Jacob wondered what he was asking that he could not put into words, only into his eyes. He thought that for the first time, despite or because of his physical wreckage, Lootjens looked like a decent human being. There was no calculation in him at this moment, no fakery, no selfishness or avarice.

"Goodbye ...my friend." Jacob said, and by the way Lootjens face lit up Jacob realized that was exactly and all he wanted to hear.

"Yes, yes, and goodbye to you, too, Jacob, my friend."

The pilot marched him down the hill, his torn rags draggling behind him, but Lootjens somehow managed to look not like an object of scorn, but rather like royalty – a man in a very select circle, Jacob's friend.

They spread a picnic on the wide flat boulder where the patio had used to be and as they ate and drank, the sacred light came on in the hermitage, slowly, minute by minute, like the rising sun.

By the next day the story was all over town

and Ezla, sitting in the tea shop by his beloved Blackie's vase, said to Anna, "I can not understand a thief who is so indiscriminate as to steal anything that is not nailed down, even dirt!"

"The love of money is the root of all evil," Anna quoted.

"I would never steal for money," Ezla said.

"No, you wouldn't steal at all," she assured him.

Ezla never was sure whether or not Anna knew he'd stolen the vase. Now was the time to tell her, to unload, but she intervened. "You would only take something you loved to fix it a little, make it more perfect, as you did with this vase of Blackie's. You are a good man, Ezla. You are our dear friend forever. And think how quickly you fixed it. I don't think it was gone for more than an hour."

"What was this Dutch man going to do with the holy man's dirt?"

"Sell it on auction over the Internet." She explained about the Internet and what went on there.

"Do you think I could find any of Blackie's pots and vases and tea sets on this Internet of yours?"

"No, Ezla. I think you pretty much have them all plus the one here that you visit. When are you going to open your Blackie's Museum by the way?"

"Soon. Very soon."

Chapter 39
The Unknowable

Two weeks passed by. Errol took the children to Ireland. Drang came on a brief visit to Anna from the capitol, taking a break from establishing a new government.

Anna officially closed the tea shop for the year to all visitors. Of course her friends among the townspeople were welcome indefinitely.

Jacob did not know when or if he would return to Austria. On his crutches he was able to go as far as the ponies' pasture and there, feeling at rest, whiled away the hours leaning on the rails, watching the ponies play their game, perhaps talking to other war veterans who liked to do the same, resting and rail-leaning. It was here that the monk, Ho, had found him after Jacob had made his confession to

Joe. Ho had given him his task. To go after Anna. To find her. To bring her back to Joe.

Jacob thought he would like to stay on in the town if he could be of some use to Anna and the children in the absence of Drang although clearly Anna didn't need her holy bodyguard anymore. Maybe he could persuade her that she needed him or, better, maybe he could persuade himself he didn't need to be needed, he could just remain out of love.

Chen also had lingered in the town but wasn't much seen by Anna or Jacob. He was choosing to be solitary, which they respected, but one day Anna came upon him by chance in the park where, as usual, she had gone to play with the children. She had a tangle of laughing children around her when she almost tripped over Chen who was sprawled on a park bench near the stone elephants, arms laid over the back of the bench, legs straight out. She had never seen him in a lounging position.

"Chen!"

"Hello, Anna," he said, sitting up straight.

"Don't get up. I'll sit beside you if I may. Run away little ones." She clapped her hands and shooed them away, then took her place on the bench.

"I have been doing what the Americans call

hanging out. This is something I have never done in all my life."

"When you refer to all your life, are we talking about decades, here, or centuries?"

Chen didn't answer. He was the master of not answering questions, but she saw a smile in his eyes. They were silent together for a while then he turned to her, saying, "I have been thinking about you, Anna, wondering if you have decided to be a holy woman or not and -- a different question entirely, perhaps a deeper one -- are you a holy woman or not."

"No to both questions. Remember after Joe's burial, and the storm, Chen, when the monks were all saying I was not a holy woman, and I stood my ground and said Joe had anointed me? Remember how they said Joe, old and failing, had seen me as his lost daughter, maybe even as his lost wife, but not really as the next holy person. It made me mad. I still don't know if they were right but I do know that on our journey together I realized Joe really loved me, deeply loved me, as the human being that I was, and that I returned his love, not because he was the holy man but because he was Joe."

Again they were silent. Then Anna continued to speak, coming closer to him, settling comfortably on the hard bench as if it were a sofa. "Chen, I don't want to be loved by hordes of people. I want to be loved by my family and friends and my lover. Yes, my lover. Everyone thinks I am all lit up and shining with glory because of an enlightenment but no, Chen, it is because of my ardent love for a man and, hopefully, for his child that is within me."

Chen smiled as she finished. "So, you see, I am not a holy woman at all. I am, as you said, or prophesied, an ordinary woman."

"Well, certainly you have answered my first question which is that you have decided not to be a holy woman. The second question is out of your hands to answer and remains to be seen. Anna, you have freed yourself from anxiety and fear. You have freed yourself from straining after holiness, you are not driven by desire for success or fear of failure - in your business or in your love life. You are responding naturally to your immediate needs without being calculating about the future. This is being a sage, Anna."

"Thank you, Chen." Again they were silent together. Anna's heart was full and it seemed that Chen's was also. "What about you, Chen? Joe cared so much about you."

"I know that. I shall not be going back to

Universe-city. I have many teachers there, lieutenants as it were, to take over for me. I always told them, You make all the minor decisions. I make all the major decisions. And there are no major decisions." Anna laughed.

"So, education will go on at my universal university, only the star will no longer give audience to the rich and famous, no longer give his weekly talks to the students and stand there in all his excellence as the god they should aspire to imitate."

"What will you do?"

"Nothing. I will begin at the beginning, with the unknowable."

"The Tao?"

"Yes. Proceeding from no place, it enters where there is no crack."

"But what about all your ..."

"Things? My cars, my planes, my city, my art and architecture? I don't have room for them on this bench."

"You don't have room for them in your new serenity," Anna said.

Chapter 40
The Holy Woman

Now Melissa, home from Ireland, was sitting on the bench with Chen, telling him a story. It was about how, in the spring time, she had gone creek-stomping with Jimmy, and gotten separated from him. She didn't feel lost because she knew to follow the creek down stream, and also because she had Bear with her, and he would know the way home. Then the creek got too deep to stomp in anymore so she crawled up the bank and pressed her way through the long grasses and bushes until finally she had no idea in the world where she was. But Bear was still with her.

Chen seemed to easily understand her words which flew from her lips, each trying to get ahead of the other, and often returning in on themselves.

He listened with interest. In the excitement of telling it all to Chen, Melissa got off the bench so she could add gestures and movement to her tale.

"Then I stumbled over something and fell down hard, getting two ow-ies on my knees. I cried, even though I knew I was being a baby, and Bear licked my tears. Then the thing I fell over kind of said something to me. It was Joe. It had his voice and smell and pretty eyes even though it was just a dirty old bundle. But I knew it was Joe and I had to bring him home." She paused, remembering back to that long ago spring that was four months ago, a huge interlude for a five year old. "It weighed a hundred pounds. I don't know how I got it on Bear's back but I did. Then I followed Bear. It took a long time. It even got dark. It was raining hard, too, I forgot about that part." She paused again, tried to elaborate on the rain but sufficed to say, "I got wet. Wetter than I got in the creek." Chen nodded. "When we got near home, Bear ran off, dropping the bundle. I had to drag it the whole rest of the way. When I got home I was so happy to see Mom I left it on the ground by the door and forgot about it. Then next morning she found it and, you know what? It was Joe's robe." A beatific smile lit her face.

Chen nodded. "I like that story. Melissa, finding that robe of Joe's was your sword-in-the-stone."

Then Chen told her the story of the boy, Arthur. "He was just a sky-larking, lovely boy full of fun who surprised everyone. There was a sword buried in a stone, all but the handle, and it was said that whoever pulled it out would become King. Arthur said he would pull the sword free and everyone laughed at him. But he did. He pulled the sword from the rock and became the king of England.

"So, little one, when I say that finding Joe's robe and lugging it home in the storm and the dark ..."

"Bear helped me!"

"Yes, he did. I know that. But the bundle was waiting for you to find it and you did the last, hard part by yourself. What it means is that you are to be the next holy man."

"No, Chen. Mom is. Because Mom was 'nointed. Anointed."

"She was anointed by Joe to raise you as only she could do. To prepare you for your great work."

"What does anointed mean, anyhow?"

"Singled out. Blessed."

"Does Mom know it was just about being a mother, after all."

"I think so."

"Will you stay here with us while I grow up?"
"Yes."
"Will you teach me the way you taught Joe?"
"Yes."
"I want to be just like Joe."
"You already are."

The End

Lightning Source UK Ltd.
Milton Keynes UK
UKHW011113260821
389520UK00001B/149